Party Planning for Murder

Books by

Michelle L. Clifton

Taryn O'Kelly Mysteries

Party Planning for Murder (Book 1)
Frost and Foul Play (Novella 1.5)
Cruises, Cocktails, and Corpses (Book 2)
Sparks, S'mores, and Scandals (Book 3)

Party Planning for Murder

Michelle L. Clifton

SaltyInspirations.com

Published in the United States by Salty Inspirations

All Salty Inspirations titles are available for purchase at Amazon .com or through SaltyInspirations.com

Library of Congress Control Number: 2024910696

ISBN: 979-8-9908817-0-9 (Paperback)

ISBN: 979-8-9908817-1-6 (Hardcover)

ISBN: 979-8-9908817-2-3 (E-pub)

Printed in the United States, Britain, Canada, & Australia.

Cover Design by Michelle Clifton

Salty Inspirations

Cape Coral, FL 33904

www.saltyinspirations.com

Second Edition: January 2026

For my amazing family!

I am forever blessed!

Chapter 1

There is nothing more relaxing than sitting on my balcony with my French-style patio furniture, overlooking the beautiful Winterburn River. With a cup of coffee and my laptop, I can peacefully sit and plan the next great event. If you're wondering what in the world I'm talking about, I am an event coordinator. I plan parties of all sorts, from weddings and anniversaries to company parties and birthdays. If you have anything to celebrate, I, Taryn O'Kelly, am the girl for you. Today, however, I sit thinking of how to plan a wedding for probably my most impossible client yet, Marcy Miller. She's one of those people where no matter what you do, you're always wrong, even to the point that if she's done something wrong, she will still find a way to blame it on you.

You're probably thinking why don't I decline the offer? Well, my number one reason is I really need the money, but secondly, she's marrying my best friend's cousin, who just happens to be well on his way to becoming a millionaire.

The event alone will pay my rent for six months, not to mention all the publicity I will get. I could really use a high-profile event like this. I've only been in business one year now, and if I want to keep my patio/river muse, I have got to start making some serious money.

Kandice, my best friend, got me the job. We have been friends since kindergarten and pretty much inseparable since. She and I used to work together at Dr. Raymond's as orthodontist assistants. I quit, not because I didn't enjoy the job, but I longed for adventure and freedom from the 8-5. Plus, planning and organizing things are like heaven to me. I know, I'm a special kind of crazy, but I can't help it. The feeling I get when I plan something to perfection is indescribable. So, I took the little bit of savings I had and started Amazing Memories, Planning Your Best Memories the Easy Way, and I haven't looked back since.

I was relaxing in a bit of a daze, enjoying the warming summer air, when my phone rang, disturbing my peace. Only one week after taking on Marcy's wedding, she was calling like a madwoman at 7:30 in the morning.

"Hello Marcy. How are you?" I said in the most cheery voice I could muster.

"Not well at all!" she whined. "I have not heard from you in hours. Where are my venues to look at? I can't sit here all day wondering where I'm going to be married!"

"Marcy, we only narrowed it down last night. It's not even 8:00 yet, and I still need a date. I can't get you a guarantee on a place until we have a date. This way we can make sure they are available."

"I gave you a date already; I know I told you, it's going to be October 1st."

"Great! Now we are rolling. How about I call you after I have spoken to them all and set up appointments? In the meantime, get your guest list together, and we can send out some of those save the date magnets you liked by the end of the week."

"Okay, you call me, but if I don't hear from you by lunchtime, I will be calling again. I mean, honestly Taryn, we only have four months."

"I'll do my best Marcy, talk to you soon. Bye."

Ugh! Do you see what I mean? She's crazy. I'm glad it's only going to be four months of this. Oh, and for the record, she did not have a date as of 6:00 last night.

I spent the rest of the morning tidying up existing clients' events and scheduling appointments at various places to hold the Miller/Peterson wedding. Before Marcy could call again, I called her and let her know the times and venues we would be visiting this week. The first two were scheduled for this afternoon. She insisted that she drive. I wasn't sure I wanted to get into a vehicle with that crazy control freak behind the wheel. However, duty calls, and so do the bills. So, I reluctantly agreed. She can't be all bad, right? She is the bride, and the term Bridezilla isn't around for nothing. Maybe she is really sweet, just not while planning her wedding.

She pulled up to the house while I was still having lunch. Ugh... she's early.

"Hi Marcy," I said as I opened the door. "Ready to make this real?" This was one of my favorite parts of planning, picking out where to have the party. It was like a blank canvas for me to paint on!

"Um. It is real! That's why I have this," she said, wiggling her fingers at me. Flashing her huge one-carat diamond, with several smaller diamonds lining the band, engagement ring at me. "You'll understand if you ever get a ring," she said.

She sure knows how to take the wind out of your sails. And did I mention how big the ring was? Oh, and I *had* a ring once before; the ring-giver just didn't have me. Sheesh.

"Okay, Marcy, let me grab my stuff and we can go."

Our first stop was The Old Victorian Bed and Breakfast. The place was a renovated Victorian home on a very large plot of land near the town center of Silver Springs. It was one of the first homesteads of Silver Springs. The Rocky Creek that feeds the Winterburn River ran through its beautifully landscaped yard of aspen groves and flower gardens featuring every color of the rainbow throughout the seasons.

We walked up the steps onto a covered wrap-around porch and knocked on the bright blue door. Tom, the owner, answered. Tom was a handsome man in his late fifties; he had a large frame, salt and pepper hair, dark eyes, and a gentle smile.

"Ms. O'Kelly," he said, "so nice to see you again, planning another wedding, I see."

"Yes, this is Marcy Miller; she is the bride to be."

Tom stuck out his hand. "Nice to meet you, Miss. Well, let's get straight to it."

He stepped out, closing the door behind him.

"Follow me around the porch. We'll look at where the ceremony would be held first. I find that is what interests most brides above all else."

We followed him down the steps and walked along a stone pathway, making our way to a flat grassy area where they held the ceremonies. The gardens were overflowing with spring flowers: purple bearded irises, pink lilies, red poppies, and a few leftover yellow daffodils. Some annuals had already been planted too. Multi-colored pansies and petunias lined the path.

Marcy was her usual annoying self; her nasal voice irritated my ears.

"My, are these flowers going to be able to last until October?"

"No, Miss," Tom replied. His voice was soft and caring. "These won't; this is our late spring-early summer cycle. The gardens are planted in seasonal cycles. The flowers will be different, but they will be just as beautiful this fall as they are now. The color scheme and flower texture will be different, of course. We will have various shades of yellow, orange, red, and purple, and more from the mum and daisy family."

"I knew that," Marcy snapped back at him as though she had never asked for his input in the first place.

I shrugged my shoulders and motioned that she was crazy. He nodded and continued down the path. Once we reached the grassy area, Marcy gasped! "This is gorgeous; we would be married right along the river!"

I told her to envision a white archway right in front of the river with crimson red Virginia creepers flowing over it. It would match the maple trees that bordered the edge of the grass just before the lot became a small forest. We could have two gold and cream swirled vases at the base of the archway, one on each side. They could be filled with green foliage and roses of all colors, with three white calla lilies in the center to represent the past, the present, and the future.

"Oh, that would be wonderful!" She clasped her hands together and did a little bounce.

Great, I thought, maybe this won't be so bad after all.

"We could set up elegant canopies above the white chairs for the guests. Each chair could have golden back covers, and in the aisle, we could lay a cream-colored strip of fabric leading to the altar."

Marcy was beside herself with all of my ideas and didn't seem to have anything rude or annoying to say, so I suggested we go inside and look at where the reception could be held.

Once inside, we toured the house, and she found it to be every bit as beautiful as the gardens. The house had a great dining room, a sitting room, and five bedrooms all themed with events that tied into the Victorian era. The guests would be able to roam the house since the whole house would be rented out for the wedding. The only problem I saw with the house was that it would be hard to have a sit-down dinner with the number of people Marcy had planned on inviting. I figured I would cross that bridge later. No sense in crossing it now if I may not ever need to.

Marcy had seen what she needed and was ready to leave, so we thanked Tom for the tour and let him know that we would be in touch by the end of the week.

Once in the car, Marcy was babbling and overflowing with excitement, and that had only been our first stop. We drove about twenty minutes out of town to Crystal Lakes Estate, our second stop. As we pulled up to the Estate Marcy gasped. The house was a mini-mansion. It was approximately 12,000 square feet, and the grounds were perfectly manicured. It was like driving up to a movie set and expecting to see Time Magazine's sexiest man of the year come out. The driveway curved into a circle, and in the center was a pond with a statue of Aphrodite pouring water from a vase into it. The pond was filled with large coy and lily pads. The house was beige stone resembling marble; it had an Italian villa meets castle look.

We rang the bell, and a tall thin man, by the name of Sam, opened the door. He was dressed in a black suit, complete with a tie. Far too hot for the beginning of summer, I thought.

"Hi, I'm Taryn O'Kelly and this is Marcy Miller. We have an appointment to look at the grounds to see if this is where the Miller/Peterson wedding will be held."

"Ah yes, Miss O'Kelly, come in," he said. His voice was gruff and assertive, not what I'd expected to come out of his frail-looking body.

"Come into the tea room while I get Mrs. Williams. I assume she is the one you spoke to?"

"Yes sir, she is," I said. Probably a little too formal, but he seemed to command it. Marcy looked at me with curious eyes.

"This is a beautiful house, but doesn't it feel strange, too quiet, maybe? And that man, he's weird." Marcy's nasally voice grated on my ears. However, she was right; the house did feel strange. I had never been here before. The only reason I knew about this place was from a brochure that had been sent to me this spring. It was advertised as a perfect location to host weddings, complete with a horse-drawn carriage if you desired. I had put the brochure in my venue binder; Marcy had been the first customer to show serious interest. She had more money to spend than most of my clients.

"I think it feels strange because the house is not currently rented out to anyone. It's so big you expect a bustling household."

Marcy rolled her eyes at me and sighed, "Obviously."

Just when you think you can tolerate her, maybe even befriend her? She pulls crap like that. I just wanted to smack her. Count to ten, Taryn, I told myself. I'm Irish American; I can tolerate my liquor very well, but I do not do so well with my temper. Before I could say anything I regretted, a voice came from the doorway.

"Hello ladies, can I get you anything? Scones, coffee, or tea?"

I looked up to see who I assumed was Mrs. Williams. She was a short, plump woman with a cheery tone to her voice. Her dark curly hair was graying, and she looked a lot like Grandma Nut from Candy Land. She was wearing a flower-print dress and a little white apron.

"The scones are fresh from the oven," she said. "I just finished making them."

"Hi, I'm Taryn and this is Marcy, the bride-to-be. You must be Mrs. Williams?" I stuck out my hand.

"Yes, you are correct deary. Now, how about I get you girls something before I show you the grounds?"

"I'll have a coffee and a scone, please."

"Me too," Marcy said.

Mrs. Williams came back with a tray of blueberry scones and a pot of coffee. While we drank our coffee and ate our scones, Mrs. Williams told us all about what Crystal Lakes Estate could provide. She let us know that the estate was owned by a very wealthy businessman who vacationed here throughout the year. His name was Rich Myers, and he hoped the house would bring as much joy to those who rented it as it did to him when he was here.

The house had eight rooms each with its own bathroom, a huge dining hall, a tea room, a cinema room, a chef's kitchen, and an office for employees only.

Before Mrs. Williams had finished her spiel, Marcy had consumed two cups of coffee and four scones. She said all this planning was making her hungry. I didn't ask, nor did I really care if she ate the whole tray. I just wanted to get moving so I could be rid of her sooner.

"Okay, ladies, let's take a look at where the wedding would be held. Right this way out to the back patio."

The patio was made of redwood, Trex decking, and the patio furniture looked like a large living room set. The cushions on the patio set were cream-colored with a bold red striping pattern, and the frame had a dark wood finish. Flower baskets were positioned neatly at the corners of the deck; and they were spilling over with petunias, pansies, marigolds, and other annuals. They might make it until October, I thought, if it doesn't freeze hard before that. The view from the patio was breathtaking; it looked out onto a small lake and further past to the Caraway Mountains. We took the three steps down from the deck and stood on the thick green lawn, gazing out onto the lake for a moment. Marcy seemed to be speechless. Unusual for her.

We wandered around the grassy area, and I spouted ideas and pointed to help enhance the picture. I talk with my hands.

"We could put a small two-step platform right in front of the lake for you, Dan, and your preacher to stand on, then a one-step on either side for the bridesmaids and groomsmen. We could still do large vases of roses and lilies and put them at the entrance of every other row where the guests will sit," I said, hoping Marcy could imagine what I was seeing in my mind.

"Ms. Miller, you could arrive by boat from across the lake," Mrs. Williams suggested. "We have a small cottage down the path alongside the lake; you could get ready for your ceremony there if you would like." Mrs. Williams pointed towards the tiny path.

"That would be great," said Marcy. "Can we go and see it now?"

We walked down the little path to the cottage. I was surprised I hadn't noticed it before, but the forest surrounding the property concealed the cottage well. It was a cute little cabin with a small porch. The front door opened onto one big room and a small loft. The big room consisted of a kitchenette, a living room with a fireplace, and a bathroom. The loft was a cozy, romantic bedroom. It felt like a hidden country getaway. If I were in a relationship, this is where I'd want to spend a steamy night away from the world. It was very romantic.

"This is just fantastic," said Marcy. "We could stay here on our wedding night and be away from everyone in the house."

We walked back up to the main house.

"Is there anything else you would like to see?" asked Mrs. Williams.

Marcy shook her head, no. We thanked Mrs. Williams, and Sam the doorman led us out.

"That was perfect," Marcy said. "This is where I want to be married."

"We still have a couple of places to look at. Would you like to see them and then make your official decision?"

"I guess we can still look at the others. I just don't see any point."

"Talk it over with Dan, and we can regroup in the morning."

It was 4:30 when Marcy dropped me off at my house. I live in a two-story condo. The lower level is a one-car garage and storage, and the upper level is my living area. I have two bedrooms, one and a half baths, and a kitchen dining living room combo. I use the second bedroom as my office. The dining area has French doors that open onto my beautiful balcony overlooking the river.

As I walked up the steps to my front door, I suddenly felt drained. I could feel the need for a nice hot bath in the Jacuzzi tub and a glass of wine coming on. It would be great if I had someone to share the bath with, but I don't. Unfortunately, I plan other people's fairy tale endings, but not my own. Oh well, I guess I'll have to settle on my cat to keep me company. Giselle, my cat, always lies in the bathroom while I'm in there. She is a very soft, fluffy Maine-Coon mix.

Once inside, I quickly checked my messages; nothing that couldn't wait until tomorrow. I drew the bath and skipped the wine. It would have been nice not to go anywhere, but I promised my mother I would come to dinner.

It was 5:30 when I got out of the tub. I felt refreshed and relaxed. Almost too relaxed, I could have just got into my pajamas, but I had to be at my mom's by 6:00. She's only a ten-minute drive from my house, and that's when the traffic was bad. So, I had plenty of time to get ready.

I pulled on my white cargo capris and put a pink tee on; hand-scrunched my auburn hair and coated my eyelashes with some mascara. I slipped on my flip-flops and was ready to go. I have very fair skin, think glow stick, but since the invention of spray tanning, my complexion has a slight caramel tone. This allows me to wear less makeup when I don't feel like taking the time. 5:50 pm, time to go. I said goodbye to my cat and ran down the steps to my car. I took 17th to Main, turned onto 12th Street, and went two blocks up to 3rd Avenue. My parents live in the historic district of Silver Springs. The houses in their neighborhood were built in the mid to late 1800s.

Chapter 2

As I arrived at the steps of my parents' two-story Victorian home, I could already hear the laughter pouring from the old house. It's seen a lot of family gatherings and holds some of my best childhood memories. The house has been in the family for four generations, and I hope it always will be.

Dinner with my family is always a little crazy and a whole lot of fun. This is especially true if you like a good bottle of wine and listening to Gramma's stories about three times over before the evening is done. That may sound crazy, but with a glass of wine under your belt, it gets to be hilarious. Gramma's 76 years old, has a small thin frame that barely sprouts 5'2" from the ground, slightly graying red hair, and is still a ball of Irish fire. She has deep green eyes and seems to know things before they happen. I think I'm most like her than anyone else in my family, except for her seemingly clairvoyant ability; the closest I've ever come to a premonition is the cramping sensation I get before my monthly cycle starts. Anyhow, it's a start, right?

My brother, Scotty, opened the door before I had a chance to get up to it. He is older than me by two years, and he is 6'5" which makes him nearly a foot taller than me. He has always been a comedian; he actually does comedy acts downtown two nights a week. The rest of the time, he is a firefighter. The fact that he is older and a lot taller makes him think he has the right to harass me.

"Come here, little sis, and give me a hug. I haven't seen you in a while."

I'd barely got in the door before he'd picked me up, spun me around, and squeezed the breath out of me.

I coughed as he sat me down. "I've been very busy with my job here lately, and to top that, one of my current clients is a huge pain in the butt. I bet she's leaving me messages as we speak. Life is rough as a business owner."

"Yeah, tell me about it. The comedy gig is killing me. I've been asked to do a third night a week, but with the hours I put in at the fire department, I'm not sure I want to try to swing it."

"So, what are you going to do?"

He shrugged his shoulders. "Eh, not worry about it and see what happens," he said.

There's another big difference between Scotty and me. He is a fly by the seat of his pants kind of guy, and well, I would plan every minute of every day if I could. As it is, I plan out all the details of my life within my control. I only wish I could control more.

"Taryn's here everyone, we can eat!" Scotty said as we walked through the entryway towards the dining room.

"Come to the table," announced my mother. I went to the kitchen and helped carry out the meatloaf and baked macaroni and cheese. This is one of my favorite meals. My mom loves to cook. She makes nearly everything from scratch, and it tastes so good. She recently updated her kitchen into a chef's dream world. Lots of counter space, all stainless steel appliances, and a gas cooktop on the island. To keep a little of the old Victorian feel, she had all the original woodwork refinished, chose cabinets that matched and painted them a creamy soft yellow, and painted the walls a cornflower blue. She also has a little breakfast nook that looks out to the backyard.

As we gathered around my mother's old oblong table, the clanking of the plates being served up almost overcame the noise of my family. Almost. Gramma and Gramps live here with Mom and Dad, part of the deal with the house being handed down. My uncle Patrick and his wife, Suzy, live a couple of blocks over and were lucky enough to buy their house before the market skyrocketed. He is my mother's brother. They get together about every other week for dinner and see each other practically daily for coffee. I try to make it as much as possible. Probably not enough for my family, but they understand. They are all mostly retired, so they have a lot of time on their hands.

"So, Taryn, how's work?" my mother asked.

"Oh, it's fine Mom, I just got a client whose wedding should really help my business out."

"Well that's nice, have you found a nice young man yet?"

"No, I've been pretty busy."

"Too busy to look for a husband? What about all those groomsmen you meet? There has to be someone you're interested in?"

"No, Mom, not really, besides it is probably not a good idea to hit on my clients' friends."

"You haven't decided to swear off men again, have you? Oh, please tell me you aren't gay now."

"No, Mom, I'm not gay. I just haven't found the right guy yet."

"You do know you have to date men to find the right one," my dad said.

"Thanks, Dad, can we change the subject now?" Everyone stared at their plates, looking a little uncomfortable. Did I mention earlier that my family keeps no secrets, even at the cost of individual embarrassment? Mom's happy for me starting a business; she just worries that I won't take time to have a family. The family thing is all she's ever done.

Dinner was pretty quiet after that, just the clanking of forks against the plates. They were all probably wondering if I was a closet gay. Uncle Patrick's two kids, my cousins, are married, and each has a kid. My mom can't wait for grandchildren, and my brother is a hopeless cause, so that leaves me as the target. She was married to my father at the age of 20 and had my brother and me by the time she was 24.

The thing is, I was close to being married about two years ago and would have been happy to produce those greatly wanted grandchildren. But a few months before the wedding, Kandice, Robert, my ex, and I were in Las Vegas; and I found him sleeping with some stripper in our hotel room. He had picked her up while Kandice and I were out looking at wedding dresses. Nice right? Anyway, he made some excuse that he couldn't help himself; the stripper made him need her. Blah blah blah. I told him cheating was cheating, and that I doubted that she had any real control over his pants. Nonetheless, we ended our relationship there. The best part is that Kandice and I left him in Las Vegas, letting him find his own way home. After that, I went on a short rant about hating men and how I would never get married. But time has healed that wound and then some. The fact is, I would love to meet a nice guy, get married, and have kids.

After dinner, the hostile environment had changed back to the fun-loving family I adore. We played card games and had dessert. My mom makes dessert several times a week, and today she made a chocolate cake with fudge frosting. My gramma reminisced about her childhood, telling us all how she used to go to the movies for a nickel and watch the old Abbott and Costello shows. She and her friends would spend hours laughing at those shows. Or the time when they tried to play Superman off the barn lofts into the hay wagons. I thought about what it would have been like to live in those carefree times without the constant interruptions of technology. Sometimes, I wish I had lived back then. Except when she talks about the outhouse they had and how they washed their clothes by hand in a bucket. That's when I am happy to have too much technology interrupting my day.

It was getting late, I was tired and had just lost my third round of Spite and Malice. I didn't want to leave my mom with a mess, so I walked around scooping up dessert plates and helped her clean up the kitchen.

"Well, family, I must get going now," I announced and made my rounds dishing out hugs and kisses, "until next time. Love you all. Bye."

On my drive home, I thought about what my mother had said and wondered if I was unconsciously still mad at men. It had been nearly two years, and I hadn't really dated anyone. I assured myself that she was wrong, and that I was just much too busy with my new business. However, maybe I would try harder to find someone.

I woke up at 3:00 in the morning, my mind racing with the events that had led up to my current single status. It wasn't my fault he couldn't keep his appendage in his pants, and why was this bothering me now? After tossing and turning for about an hour, I decided to get up; I obviously wasn't going back to sleep and needed to clear my head. I worked on a couple summer picnics I had to wrap up for a couple of companies, and at about 5:30 I thought I'd go for a run.

Silver Springs has a beautiful paved trail that runs along the river through town. I dressed in my usual running attire of a pink sports bra and purple razorback top, black running shorts, Adidas running shoes, and a ponytail. Oh, and my .380 pistol, aka the Cricket, neatly tucked into the small of my back beneath my shorts. My dad and brother both hunt and do competition shooting. They weren't about to let me get by without knowing how to use a gun. Besides, we have really big bears here. I've never needed to use it, but my dad always says better to be safe than sorry. So, I usually pack it along wherever I go.

The air was cool and crisp; the sun was just starting to touch the path, and I ran at a nice even pace, thinking and trying to clear my thoughts with the sweet fresh air. It smelled like the ice-cold river; I could hear it roaring past me. Not many people were on the river walk yet this morning, but by mid-morning it would become a bustling place with families on bike rides, fellow runners, kids on the way to the pool, and pet owners out with their furry friends. I love it down here; it's so peaceful.

As I was running along on my way home, someone came at me from behind the bushes. I heard the voice say something about a little outfit and wanting something. A hand grabbed my arm. I yelled and pulled my gun on him, and then I realized who it was.

"Robert? What in the hell are you doing? You scared the crap out of me." I lowered my gun. "I could have shot your ass. Why would you jump out at me like that? Are you trying to give me a heart attack?"

He looked at me with those puppy-dog eyes, and it made me feel uncomfortable.

"Don't look at me that way, Robert."

"You used to like it," he said.

I glared at him. "Not anymore! What were you doing in the bushes, Robert?"

"I was thinking. Thinking about you and how I wish things had turned out differently."

"More like how you wish you hadn't been caught."

"Well yes, that too, but I told you why I did it."

"Oh, yeah, because when she swung her ass at you, that was her way of telling you she needed you. I had almost forgotten that none of this was your fault. How many other women's needs did you fulfill while we were together?"

"Do you really want to know?" He looked at me, puzzled.

"What? No! Agh! I didn't mind the women who would idly flirt with you when we were together because I thought you only had eyes for me. I felt so lucky to have a guy who knew he was so good-looking, who could have anyone he wanted, and he chose me. I'm sorry I ever thought that you would only choose me. You see someone move slightly provocatively, and you take it as a need to fill their inner desire. What I can't figure out is how I, and so many others, actually bought your smooth-talking crap in the first place."

"Oh, Taryn, calm down. You used to be so much more fun," he said as he grabbed my shoulders.

"Yeah, back when your dirty tricks worked on me. Go away, Robert." I shoved him off me.

"But baby, I miss you, and I have changed."

"Yeah, because jumping out of the bushes at me and scaring the crap out of me is proof of your new ways. You ended it for us when you found the stripper who needed you so badly. GoodBye Robert!" I turned and ran off.

How could he be such a jerk? If he weren't so damn cute, it would be a lot easier. Robert was a tall and charming man with blond hair and dark, alluring eyes. He had a killer smile that showed off his perfectly tanned skin. There's just one problem: you can't trust him as far as you can throw him, and for a 110-pound woman like myself, that's not far.

Once home, I was furious at the nerve of him. The last time I saw him was at a mutual friend's Christmas party. He had some bimbo hanging on him, so I didn't have much contact with him. That was fine with me. Ah… I needed a hot shower and some coffee, quick. Why did I have to see him today? My life was moving along just fine. I admit that I do not love him now. How could I? But seeing him again was hard. He is so freaking good-looking, and we had some really good times together. It's been two years, maybe there is something wrong with me. I thought about calling Kandice, but she would be on her way to work by now, so I texted her instead, asking her to go to lunch with me today.

I worked a little more on a few accounts that needed my attention. I had an engagement party, a 50th wedding anniversary, and a couple of Fourth of July parties to do.

I decided I had better check my messages since I hadn't answered any calls today. I had a message from my mom asking me to call her. A message from a client thanking me again for the wonderful graduation party I had done for her, and of course, one from Marcy. She wanted to make sure that I had not canceled the other appointments this week. She needed to see them before she and Dan could make a decision. I'd better call her back now or my voicemail will blow up.

"Marcy, hi, it's Taryn. How are you?"

"Well, I could be better. You didn't answer this morning, and I was getting a little worried that you might have canceled my appointments. Oh, tell me you didn't cancel them."

"No, Marcy, of course not. I won't do anything until I okay it with you first. We are still on for Thursday to see our last two stops."

"Okay Taryn, I just wanted to be sure. I'll see you Thursday."

"Okay, bye."

That deed was done, and I had a few other things to finish up.

It was finally lunchtime, and Kandice had texted me back, asking me to meet her at Pepe's for lunch. Pepe's is an Italian café with a great patio and awesome panini sandwiches. I decided to walk; I was in no mood to try to find parking downtown. When I arrived, Kandice had not made it yet, so I sat at one of the patio tables facing the park. A waitress by the name of Sunnie came by and recited the day's specials and then handed me their lunch menu. I let her know I was expecting a friend and ordered two iced teas. As I waited for Kandice, sipping on the tea Sunnie had brought, I noticed a very handsome man sitting at the table next to me.

"Hey, didn't your mother ever teach you that staring is rude? Are you drooling?"

I looked up to see Kandice with a huge grin on her face. "I wasn't staring or drooling — ah, who am I kidding? I was, but look at him; how could you not?"

Kandice looked over. "Damn, girl, he's going to make me drool."

"I saw him first!"

"Calm down, Fido."

"Oh, I'm sorry, I had a morning from hell."

"I figured as much when I got your text. Let's order; I'm starved, then you can tell me what happened."

Sunnie came back to take our order. Kandice ordered the chicken Alfredo, half size, and a salad, and I ordered the chicken and roasted red pepper panini and a salad. While waiting for our food, I filled Kandice in on my latest Robert encounter.

"What the hell was he doing in the bushes?"

"I don't know; that's what I asked him."

"This doesn't make any sense. It's been almost two years, and suddenly he wants to get back together. Don't tell me you want him back!"

"I know, I don't want him back. It just threw me for a loop today."

"Honey, you can't take him back. I won't allow it; you're better than that. Besides Mr. Hotpants over there may be on the market, I still don't see anyone with him."

"I'm not going to walk over there and ask him for his phone number. How pathetic will that look?"

"No, but I will," Kandice said, with a devilish grin.

"No, you can't do that; I'll look even more pathetic; this isn't junior high. I can't send you in to do my dirty work."

"Do you want him or not? Because if you don't, I might have to add him to my backup list."

"Backup list, what are you talking about?"

"My backup list. Right now I'm dating this guy named Trey. I met him a couple of nights ago, but if that doesn't work out, Mr. Hotpants over there could be up next. So you want him or not?"

"Well, he does look yummy."

"Honey, are you going to eat him or date him?"

"Look who's talking. You're the one who's ready to line him up for next week's menu. Maybe I should just forget about it. He's too good-looking to be single anyway, and besides, I know all this yummy talk was brought on by none other than my lousy ex. I need to focus on work."

"You always say that."

I wanted the spotlight off of me so I asked about this new guy Kandice has met. "Tell me about your new guy".

"I will, but I know what you're up to, we're not finished with Mr. Hotpants. His name is Trey, and he is self-employed, I'm not really sure what he actually does though. He's new in town and handsome in that rugged outdoors man kind of way. He is six foot, dark skin, built like a rock, and has these amazing green eyes. We are going sailing on the lake this Saturday."

"Wow! Kandice, it sounds like this one could be perfect, that is a pretty cool first date." Most men that Kandice has dated have been jerks, nice to look at but that's about it. They don't tend to keep a job, they usually drink too much, and most of them expect you to sleep with them by the third date. Not that Kandice has a real problem with that, it's just that it has to be on her terms. She totally wears the pants in her relationships.

"Now back to Mr. Hotpants over there, here's the plan. You're going to get up and go to the bathroom, on your way back you're going to 'accidentally' sit in the vacant seat across from him. Pretend you're texting someone that way it will look like a real accident, once there, flirt and talk to him."

"Okay, what's your part of the plan?"

"I'm going to make sure he doesn't leave before you get back."

"That's it? Great. Well, here goes nothing." I got up, walked past his table, and went to the restroom. That was good because I really did need to go. I had way too much ice tea with lunch. I got to the restroom, ran my fingers through my hair to fluff it up a bit, and added a little bit of pink lip gloss to my plump lips. I looked at myself in the mirror and told myself I could do this. I didn't usually go after guys; I let them be the ones to ask me out. I guess

I'm a little old-school like that. That's probably why I haven't had many guys in my life. Kandice would walk right up to a guy and tell him that they were going to go out. It usually worked for her too. But then again she looks like a dark Grecian Goddess. She is a half African American and a half Italian woman, she is 5'9, a size D cup, and size 4 waist, long wavy dark brown hair, and brown eyes. She is gorgeous.

I came out, as planned, pretending to text someone important. I tried to look business-like and not like some young, dumb, airhead. As I approached his table, my stomach was in knots. He really was incredibly handsome with thick dark hair, big, strong hands, dark honey-colored eyes, caramel skin, and an amazing smile. I could depict well-defined muscle under his green dress shirt. Oh damn, I think I started to drool again. I weaved my way around the tables and landed as planned in the chair across from him. I looked up, pretending to be startled.

"Oh, sorry I..."

"That's Okay Miss?"

"Taryn, Taryn O'Kelly." I put out my hand, and he took it in his. His hand swallowed mine; it was so warm and soft. He brought my hand up to his lips and kissed it. I'm guessing this is a good thing? His lips felt smooth and warm.

"Sorry, again Mr...?"

"Alexander Cruz, but call me Alex."

"Well, Alex, sorry again." I started to get up.

"Won't you have a seat?"

"Well, I..." Kandice motioned for me to sit, gave me the thumbs ups, and then waved me a "call me later sign". She picked up her purse and left.

"So Miss O'Kelly, what do you do for a living?"

"I'm an event coordinator, and yourself?"

"I'm a pilot for a charter company; a buddy of mine is trying to convince me to make Silver Springs my home. If I do that, I'll probably join the Police Reserve."

"Where do you currently live?"

"Denver."

"Are you here to look for a place?"

"Well, yes and no, I am here on business, but while I wait to fly my client home I have been looking."

"There's a condo for sale by my place. I think it's a reasonable price. I'll give you the address so you can go look at it if you want."

"Why don't you just show me where it is?"

"Um, I could do that." My stomach flip-flopped with excitement! "Did you drive or walk here? I walked."

"I walked too; I'm staying at Mabel's House Hotel."

"Great, the condo is not far from here. Let's go."

Chapter 3

The summer sun felt so warm on our backs as we walked. Alex had given me his arm and I couldn't help but think once again how hot he was. The heat I felt from both him and the sun made me glad I had chosen to wear a sundress today. We talked about my job, about living in Silver Springs, and about the various likes and dislikes we each have. Once we arrived at the condos, I showed him the one that was for sale. He took one of the real estate papers. He seemed to like it. I secretly hoped so; maybe we would see more of each other then. He walked me to my house and took my hand and kissed it again, sending a hot flash throughout my entire body. Oh boy, this one could be dangerous, I thought.

"Thank you, Taryn, for allowing me to enjoy your company this afternoon. I would like it if you would give me the pleasure of seeing you again sometime."

How could I resist? "I would like that too, Alex. How long are you in town?"

"Just until Friday," he said. "Are you doing anything tomorrow night?"

"No."

"May I take you to dinner?"

"Yes, I would like that."

"I'll pick you up at 6:00 pm then."

"It's a date!" How stupid did that sound, I thought? I did a mental head slap and hoped that he didn't think that it sounded as stupid as I did.

"Until tomorrow," he said. He turned and walked away.

I watched as his cute butt moved from my sight. I climbed the steps to my door and went in to find my cat at the back door meowing to go out. "All right, all right, you can go out." After letting Giselle out, I listened to my messages. Of course, Marcy had left a message letting me know that time was ticking and that I needed to call ASAP. I'll call her later; I didn't want to talk to her right now. I still hadn't called my mother back from this morning. I thought I better get that over with and then I'd deal with Marcy.

"Hi, Mom."

"Taryn, I was getting ready to call you again. I was worried about you. With the way things went last night, I thought you might be upset."

"No, Mom, I just didn't know what to do, but the good news is now I do. I have a date tomorrow night with a very nice gentleman."

"Gentlemen? He's not your father's age, is he?"

"No, Mom, he's probably about my age, maybe a little older. He's just very polite and handsome. You should be happy I'm dating again."

"Oh, Taryn, that's wonderful! When are you bringing him by?"

"I don't know; I have to get through the first date, and did I mention that he currently lives in Denver?"

"He doesn't live here? How is that going to go anywhere? I want grandchildren, you know."

"Mom, he's looking to move here very soon."

"That's great. Bring him over as soon as you can. I can't wait to meet him."

"Okay, Mom, I've gotta go. More work to get done."

"One more thing, Taryn honey, I am very proud of you. You know that, right? I just want to see you happy in all aspects of your life."

"I know, Mom, I'm working on it. Love you."

"Love you too, honey, bye."

Before I could dial Marcy's number, there was a knock at my door. I didn't have any appointments this afternoon. I wonder who that could be? Maybe it's Alex! I half-skipped to the door only to find out it was Robert.

"Ugh! How many times must I see you in one day?" I said as I answered the door.

"Well, Taryn, aren't you rude to your guests?" he said as he pushed his way inside.

"Guests? Guests! You wouldn't be a guest at my funeral. I'd haunt you just to get you to leave if you did show up."

"Feeling feisty today, Taryn? I always did like that Irish temper of yours, so sexy."

"Robert, what do you want?"

"It's like I said this morning, I'm miserable without you and I'm here to take you back."

"Take me back? Me? Who left who? I don't want you back."

"Here," he said, handing me a single red rose. "You used to like it when I brought you flowers."

"Yeah, that was before I found out what you were really like."

He walked around my house mumbling about all our good times together and touching all my stuff. I was actually impressed with some of the things he remembered, but not impressed enough to take him back.

"Robert, what are you up to? It's been nearly two years, and suddenly you're lost without me. I know you don't have trouble filling your bed, so what is it really? If you want money, I don't have any." As I said it, I knew it couldn't be true. Robert was loaded; his parents blessed him with a trust fund. I often wished I could have been so lucky.

"Taryn, you know I don't need money. I need love, your love."

"Sorry, Robert, I don't love you anymore, and you need to be going," I said as I pushed him out the door and quickly locked it before he could try to come back in.

Man, I must have done something wrong in a past life to deserve having to deal with him not once but twice in one day. I didn't know if I had the energy to deal with Marcy too. I needed chocolate to help me through this. I always kept a stash of orange cream-filled chocolates hidden in my room; they are my favorite. I grabbed a couple of those and picked up the phone to call Marcy back.

"Marcy, hi it's Taryn."

"Oh hi, Taryn, I'm in the middle of a massage, stress of planning the wedding and all. I hold all my stress in my shoulders, and the only way to relieve it is twice-weekly massage."

"You can call me back later," I said.

"Oh no, I just wanted to check in with you. Dan and I will be heading home on Friday, and I want to make sure that we can tie up the loose ends down here before I go. I think we should be able to handle a lot of it over the phone, and I'll be making trips every other week or so."

"Yes, Marcy, we will definitely be able to make all that work. I have Thursday set aside just for you."

"Great Taryn, I need to get back to my massage. Bye."

I sent Kandice a text telling her to come over for dinner and that I had a date with Alex tomorrow. It was already 4:00 pm, so I decided I'd start cooking dinner now. I looked over at my calendar to check what tonight's menu was supposed to be. Chicken enchiladas, yum, that sounded good and I knew Kandice liked them. I had pre-cooked the chicken on Sunday, so all I had to do was shred it and fill my tortillas. I filled a wine glass with a white Riesling and put on some Dean Martin to enjoy while I cooked. The enchiladas were in the oven by 4:45 pm and would be ready by the time she walked in the door. I chopped the lettuce, tomato, and purple cabbage, peeled the avocado, and set out the sour cream. The table was perfectly set. As the oven timer beeped, I heard Kandice knock and enter.

"Mmm, something smells good. Taryn, your mother's right; you need to have some kids; you're such a homemaker."

"Thanks, I think."

I filled our wine glasses, and we sat at the table; before our plates were dished, Kandice wanted to know all about Mr. Hotpants. I gave her the rundown on how things went; our walk home, his interest in the condo, how he kissed my hand and asked me out.

"Wow! He sounds smooth."

"What?" My face flushed.

"He knows how to work women."

"No, that's not what you're supposed to think. I don't want another Robert."

"Taryn, it's okay, just because he's charming and knows his way to a woman's heart doesn't mean he'll be like Robert. I never said he was a pig."

"Now you've got me worried."

"Look at it this way; he's hot and you need someone to pull you back into the game. He obviously liked you; he made up the condo showing as an excuse to spend a little more time with you. That's always a good sign."

"I guess you're right. I will definitely go on this date."

"Damn right you will!"

"Guess who else showed up today?" I took a sip of wine, "Robert."

"What? Why? Does he want me to kick his ass?"

"He's still claiming that he has changed and his life is over unless I'm in it."

"Good riddance then."

"Kandice!"

"What! I don't care if he falls off the face of the earth. He's a pig, Taryn, I thought we went over this already."

"I know, I know, you're right. On another subject, your cousin Dan is in for a real treat once he marries Marcy. She's so stressed over the planning of the wedding. She has to get a massage at least twice a week. She holds her stress in her neck and shoulders, you know. Just like every other person I know. She talks like everything happens only to her."

"Dan seems to be happy with her. I don't think he cares because he plans on spoiling her."

"She will be easy to do that to as long as he can afford it."

"That shouldn't be a problem for him. Speaking of money, I'm thinking of going to school to be a dental hygienist." Kandice said taking a sip of wine.

"Really! That would be great; you can make a lot of money doing that, and you can have pretty flexible hours."

"I know. I just barely started looking into it, but I think it's something I would like to do. I'm a little worried about the cost; I might have to start stripping just to pay for everything."

"What!" I choked on my enchilada. "Are you serious? You can't be a stripper."

"Why not? They make a killing, and I think I have the figure for it." She ran her hands down her side to her waist.

"You do; it's just why would you want to show it to every man in town."

"I practically do now anyway. I might as well get paid for it."

She had a point. Kandice was promiscuous. I hated thinking it, but she was. She didn't care who she slept with. My best friend is a kind-hearted, good person; it's just that her libido couldn't adhere to her Catholic upbringing.

"Kandice, are you sure you want to expose yourself like that? At least the guys that see you now are the ones you choose, not just whoever walks in the door."

"You have a point, Taryn. I'm just not sure what to do yet. I think I would really like to be a hygienist."

"I would love you being a hygienist; think of all the time we could schedule to hang out."

"I know, right? And if Robert were to show up, I could be here to beat his ass in an instant since you won't."

"Alright, I would beat his ass if I thought it would get me somewhere. That's enough about Robert and stripping. We will find you another way to earn some extra cash, and Alex is the new guy in town."

We finished our dinner, refilled our wine glasses, and watched Fools Rush In, one of our all-time favorite movies.

Kandice left a little after nine, and I was pooped. The day had been long and somewhat emotional. I lay in bed thinking of Robert and what had happened to us. I really thought that I was over it all, but I guess seeing him without a ho attached to him made me miss him in some way. Why was I having these feelings? I had been so mad the day I found him in bed with her. I didn't want him back; I couldn't even stand to look at him. But now that it had been so long, I couldn't help but wonder if he had changed. No, Taryn, he has definitely not changed, I told myself. Guys like that don't change; that's why you're going out with Alex tomorrow night. Yes, Alex, now, I liked thinking about him; his strong biceps, those big hands, and sexy honey-colored eyes. Mmm. I bet he looks pretty good without a shirt on. I bet he looks pretty good without anything on. I drifted off to sleep, dreaming of Alex, aka Mr. Hotpants.

I woke up with a small wet spot on my pillow and a massive headache. Great, I was drooling in my sleep. I must have been dreaming of Alex. Darn, I wish I could have remembered that dream instead of those crazy ones where people you're supposed to know morph into monkeys, and your house is arranged backwards. Why is it that the easiest dreams to remember are the craziest ones, anyway? Oh, my head hurt. I think I had a little too much wine last night. I dragged myself out of bed. It was already 6:30 am, I'd have to hurry if I wanted to squeeze in my morning run. I made some coffee, took a couple of Advil, fed my cat, and went out to sit on my patio. The fresh air would do me some good, and I could be on my run by about 7:15 am if I didn't let the mild hangover get to me.

I went out for my run, as planned, and was already feeling revived; gotta love the power of coffee and sweet summer air. I ran the river walk again; it's where I usually run. I saw a few other runners, an elderly couple strolling along, and a couple of new moms with their babies snuggled into their strollers. The day looked to be a good one. It was already warming up fast, and the flowers were looking especially bright today. I couldn't help but feel excited. I wanted today to move quickly so I could get to that date with

Alex. The thought of him made me run even faster. Yes! Today would definitely be a great day!

When I got home, I showered and fixed myself a bacon, spinach, and feta omelet, orange juice, and half of an English muffin. The breakfast of champions. Giselle meowed at my feet; she was such a beggar. I tore a little piece of my omelet off and gave it to her. She loves people food, and the way I see it is pets don't live long enough to deprive them of it. We ate our breakfast, and I cleaned up the kitchen. It had been a very quiet morning, but now it was time for work. I would be spending the day with Marcy tomorrow, and I wanted to have everything go smoothly. I also wanted her to fly home on Friday and be out of my hair.

Chapter 4

I looked at my planner, I had a couple of appointments, one at 10:00am and one at 1:00pm. I quickly tidied up the place and went to my office to get out the appropriate binders for my 10 o'clock. It was a couple that wanted to have a New Year's Eve wedding. It was a little early, but they wanted to get a place booked. Weddings are my favorite thing to plan. I've planned my own about a thousand times. They are so romantic and enchanting. I placed the binders on the table along with my portfolio. On the computer, I had a slide show of several places to have weddings and some pictures of the ones I had planned.

I absolutely love my little office. It's furnished with two large, soft, beige chairs complete with silky blue pillows, an oval coffee table with a glass top, and a blond wooden desk. My curtains are a Venetian blue and tan print, and the walls are light periwinkle blue, so light they are almost white. When I draw the curtains, I can see the steps leading up to my front door. It is really convenient when I need to work at my desk because I can watch for clients to approach.

At ten minutes to 10, my doorbell rang; it was the soon-to-be Hensleys, my 10 o'clock. I opened the door and led them into the office.

"Mr. Hensley, Ms. Taylor, I stuck out my hand. I'm Taryn O'Kelly. Would you like some coffee, tea, or water?"

"No Thanks. Call me Dean," replied Mr. Hensley.

"I'll have some water," Katy Taylor said.

I went to the kitchen and quickly returned with Katy's water. I went over my fees and listed several locations for a New Year's Eve wedding. They seemed pleased, and we decided on a couple of venues to look at. I scheduled them for the beginning of the following week. They signed my contract and left with a couple of my brochures. They had a lot to think about, colors, flowers, food, and so much more.

By the time they left, it was 11:40 am , almost lunchtime. I called my mom to check in for the day. I reminded her of my date and not to call until the next morning. I didn't want her calling and leaving me a message about babies and marriage when Alex could be around to hear it. The doorbell rang; I opened it to a man holding a beautiful bouquet of flowers.

"Are you Miss O'Kelly?" the man asked?

"Yes."

"These are for you."

I brought the bouquet in and placed it on my living room table. The bouquet was a combination of giant orange and yellow Gerber daisies, light and dark pink roses, white lilies, baby's breath, and other greenery. It was so bright and colorful. I picked up the attached card and read the message. "Dear Miss O'Kelly, you are as lovely as these flowers. I look forward to seeing you tonight. Alex."

He is so sweet. I love getting flowers. I sent Kandice a picture of them. I was dancing on air during my lunch break and couldn't wait until it was time for our date.

My one o'clock was a local business family picnic to be planned for the end of August. Right on time, Mr. Write was at the house ready to plan a picnic. I went over my fees and wrote down all of his requests. He gave me budget guidelines to work within. His company owns a piece of property just outside of town, so that took care of the location for me. I love it when a company gives me the specifics and lets me handle the rest. It makes my job so much easier.

After I had finished with Mr. Write, I had an advertisement to design. I had been working on it a little here and a little there, but now it was crunch time. The ad was due next week. Silver Springs puts out a magazine with business coupons, and I wanted to be in the next mailing.

I heard a knock at the door, followed by the sound of it opening and closing. "Hello?" I stepped out of the office to see Robert walking through the entry with a vase of red roses. There had to be about twenty of them.

"Robert! What are you doing here?"

"I thought I'd bring you some expensive roses and ask you for forgiveness. How about we start all over?" He put out his hand and introduced himself as though we had never met. "Robert and your name is?"

"You know my name."

"Oh, come on, play along."

"Fine. I'm Taryn."

"Nice to meet you, Miss. May I have this dance?"

Just as I was about to say that there was no music, a string quartet entered my house and started playing a romantic waltz. My mouth must have been hanging open because Robert placed his finger on my chin and closed it. He grabbed me and we danced until the song ended. Then he leaned in to kiss me, but I dodged it just in time.

"Robert, this is all very nice; it's just that I can't do this again, not with you. I have a date tonight, and if things go well, I'll be seeing him again." Just then he must have noticed the flowers from Alex on the table because his face got bright red with jealousy, and he walked toward the flowers, picked up the card and read it.

"Robert, that's mine!" I grabbed the note out of his hand, and then his face changed. He was calm and cool again.

"Oh, I see. I'm sorry to have disturbed you, Miss O'Kelly." He turned to leave, pivoted back on his heel, grabbed, and hugged me tightly. I'm pretty sure he touched my boob.

"Can we at least be friends?" he asked.

"Well, I... I suppose, but you have to keep your hands to yourself. Friends don't grope and kiss friends."

"10-4, good buddy." He saluted me. Before he left, he picked up the roses and placed them in front of Alex's flowers, then said goodbye and walked out the door.

What is wrong with me? Why did I entertain that? Nearly two years ago, if he had done that, it would have led to a night of hot sex and the world's most perfect breakfast. Why is he doing this to me? That was so romantic, a string quartet! I realized I was talking to my cat, and she looked very responsive lying on the couch with one eye open. I moved the roses to my office and left the daisies on the living room table. I couldn't throw away perfectly good roses, but I didn't want them in plain sight when Alex walked in either.

I sent Kandice a text briefing her on the latest Robert incident and let her know I'd call when the date was over. She texted back letting me know that it better be after breakfast with Alex when I called. I laughed. She is crazy.

I've only ever been with Robert, but Kandice has been with too many to count. She loves her men. I was raised to be a good Catholic girl, and when Robert and I set a date, I ended up breaking the waiting rule, no big deal right? We were going to be married anyway. Ha. Now, I hate that mistake.

It was 4:30 pm, and Alex was going to be here at 6:00 pm. I need to hustle if I want to look good tonight. I put my hair in rollers and tried on at least six dresses before I settled on a little red spaghetti strap dress with tiered layers. It was just above the knee in length, and it had a matching red shawl. I had these cute strappy red heels to wear with it. Perfect, now for my makeup. I put on a thin line of green eyeliner to make my green eyes stand out and a little bronze eyeshadow, mascara, and blush, and I was finished. I took out the rollers and lightly sprayed the curls to hold them in place. Feeling like I had done a successful job making myself look good, I went out to sit on my patio and wait for Alex to show up.

Alex knocked on the door right at 6:00 pm. He had on black slacks, a blue dress shirt, and a tie. He looked good.

"Hi, Alex."

"Miss O'Kelly, you're breathtaking."

That made me blush. "Thank you."

He extended his arm, and we walked out to his car. He smelled so good, I could feel a rush of heat go through my body just standing next to him. He stopped at the curb and opened the car door for me.

"Thank you," I said as I got in.

We drove to a place called Penelope's; it's one of my favorites. Penelope's sits on the edge of town. It was an old colonial farmhouse, restored on the outside and remodeled to fit fifty tables on the inside. It has a huge wraparound deck.

"I hope this place is okay with you; a friend of mine recommended it," Alex said.

"I love this place."

Alex had made a reservation for us, which was always a good thing at Penelope's because if you didn't make reservations you could easily wait a couple of hours to be seated. We checked in with the maître d. He handed us off to a cute little waitress with long braided black hair and beautiful huge dark eyes. Her name was Wendy; she led us down the spiral steps to our table.

The inside of Penelope's did not look like a farmhouse. The lighting is dim, with elegant wall sconces and table candles giving the place an enchanting, romantic air. Beautifully crafted woodwork was stained a reddish color to match the hardwood floors. The tables had fresh flowers and candles circling them. They always have a pianist, and sometimes there'll be a violinist as well. The atmosphere is very private. The table Wendy took us to just so happened to be the most romantic one in the house. The table was tucked away in a cubby like a cave. It was so private that it almost felt like we were the only ones in the restaurant.

Once seated, Alex ordered a margarita on the rocks with salt, and I had an amaretto sour. We looked over the menu and ordered. Alex had the rib-eye steak smothered in a creamy mushroom sauce, and I had the pistachio-encrusted Mahi Mahi. All the meals come with a huge hand-tossed salad and rolls. As we dug into the salad, I asked how the house hunting was going.

"I get to look at the condo by your place tomorrow."

"That's great," I said excitedly.

"How has your day gone?"

"It went well; I ended up with a couple of new clients today."

"Do you plan bachelor parties?"

"Yes, I do. Not yours, I hope." I laughed awkwardly.

"Ha! No, a friend of mine is getting married."

"Ah well, I could arrange quite a fun party."

"I may have to call you."

We continued to talk, and I found out that he flies for several companies and has traveled across most of America.

"I would love to travel."

"It can get lonely sometimes, but I do love being in the air."

Once we had finished our dinner, Alex drove me home. I didn't want it to be over already, so I did what any self-respecting woman would do. I invited him up! I had no plans on sleeping with him, I assure you. I just wanted to hang out with him a bit longer.

"Would you like to come up?"

"Yes, I would like that," he replied.

"Great." My heart skipped a beat. What was I doing?

He quickly got out of the car and was around my side opening the door for me again before I hardly had time to notice. I led the way up the steps. I'm glad I only had two of those sours, or else climbing my stairs might have been difficult.

I unlocked the door with Alex close behind me. We walked into the foyer when I felt his warm hand around my waist. He pulled me in and kissed me. His lips were warm and soft against mine, and it made me feel weak in the knees.

"I had a wonderful time tonight, Taryn," he whispered into my ear and kissed me again.

"W-would you like some wine?" I asked, taking a deep breath."

"Yes, please," he replied.

I nearly ran to the kitchen and poured us some wine. When I had come back, Alex had taken his coat off and loosened his tie. Damn, did he look sexy. I handed him his wine, and we sat on the couch. He placed his glass on the coffee table and leaned into me and kissed me again, then several more times, adding a little tongue. Just when things started to heat up and hands started to wander, his phone rang. He apologized. "Work," he said and took it out to the balcony. I went to the bathroom to freshen up, and when I came out, Alex was leaning back on the couch waiting for my return.

"Alex, I really like you, but I think we need to slow down. We only just met yesterday." Damn those morals of mine.

"I'm sorry, Taryn, I should have controlled myself. I like you a lot too."

We spent the rest of the evening watching movies and talking until sometime around 1:00 am. It was so late, I told Alex to stay; he could have the couch. I brought out some extra blankets and a pillow; we kissed goodnight and went to bed.

I woke up to the smell of freshly brewed coffee and bacon. The smell lured me out of my room, and I found Alex shirtless, cooking breakfast. Wow! I had to close my mouth; he looked so good, with perfectly defined muscles and gorgeous olive skin.

"Good morning, Taryn. Did you sleep well?"

"Y-yes. You?"

"Your couch is very comfortable."

I asked myself why I had made that arrangement again. Right, morals. Ugh!

"I hope you like eggs and bacon for breakfast."

He poured me a cup of coffee, dished our plates, and escorted me to the patio.

"I leave for Denver tomorrow. Can I see you again tonight?"

"Yes, but I'll cook here tonight," I replied.

"Sounds good to me," he grinned.

"Would 6:00 pm again work for you?" I asked.

"Perfect," he said as he leaned in to kiss me.

After enjoying breakfast together, he went back to his hotel, and I had to get ready for my appointment with Marcy.

Shortly after Alex left. I heard a knock at the door; low and behold, it was Robert.

"So, friend, how was your date? It must have been good since I just saw him leave. I always loved those sexy low-cut sleep shirts you wear." I looked down and gasped quickly, closing my robe.

"What? Are you stalking me now?"

"No! I'm just being a good friend. I want to hear about your juicy date."

"I have Kandice for that, thank you. Now leave!" I slammed the door in his face and locked it. I texted Kandice, giving her a briefing on the night's events, and told her I would try to call before Alex came back over. Her only reply was, "Screw the morals tonight, and I am going to kick Robert's ass." Lovely, I have a colorful best friend.

My phone rang. It was my mom. "Hi, Mom."

"Taryn, how was your date? When are you bringing him by?"

"Slow down, Mom. The date was great, but I'm not bringing him by this time. He leaves for Denver tomorrow. If it works out the next time he's in town, I'll be sure to bring him by."

"Humph," my mom sighed.

She was not happy when I didn't go along with what she wanted. "I promise, Mom, next time he's in town."

"Okay fine, I suppose I can wait to meet the future father of my grandchildren."

"Mom, I don't even know if this is going to work out, let alone us having children. Please, Mom, be patient. I will inform you the very second this has grandchildren potential. I've gotta go, appointments all day. Bye, Mom. Love you."

"Love you too, dear."

I got ready in record time, just as Marcy pulled up. I told her I would drive today, so we piled into my blue Toyota Tundra. As I pulled out, I thought I saw Robert's red Corvette in the rearview mirror. When I looked again, it was gone. I must have been seeing things.

"Is something wrong?" Marcy asked.

"What? uh. No, sorry, I thought I saw someone."

"Well, you looked worried."

"No, I'm fine. So, the first stop is the Silver Springs Picnic Grounds." We wandered the grounds, it had a large open meadow with a thick forest surrounding it and a small creek. You couldn't see the creek from the meadow, but you could hear its rushing water. This place had great potential to host a large wedding except that you had to bring everything, including toilets. Like last time, I spouted off several ways to hold the wedding. I could tell Marcy wasn't that into this place; she liked to show off and spend money. This one could easily be a pricey, beautiful wedding, but it did not come with the fancy house.

"Well, I like it, okay, but I still think I want Crystal Lake."

"Okay, onward to our last stop, Serenity Park," I said.

The park was beautiful, with a gazebo covered in vines that turned bright red in October and rose gardens with stone pathways on either side. The guests would have to sit in the grassy area just in front of the gazebo. At least with the park, there were bathrooms. These bathrooms weren't your typical park bathroom either. They were fancy hotel-like bathrooms. No shower, but a large marble countertop, two dressing rooms, and two water closets. This place gets rented for enough events that they actually have people come in and clean before and after as part of your fees.

"You would have to have your reception outside or at another location with either the park or the picnic area."

"Well, I'm looking at two hundred-plus people, so I think I'll go with Crystal Lake; the park is beautiful, though."

"Okay then, let's head back to my place and work on some of the details."

"Let's get lunch first, then go back to your place, I'm starving," Marcy said.

We grabbed lunch at a little Mediterranean café on 2nd Street. When we had finished our meal, we went to the condo to work on reservations, guest lists, etc. By the time Marcy left, I was pooped. She was an energy sucker; she must have changed the guest list fifty times before she was satisfied. And with every change she made, I should have already done it before she told me. Ugh! Marcy was a likable but hateable person all wrapped in one petite little package. Dan had his work cut out for him.

She rented Crystal Lake for two weeks before the wedding through two days after. She wanted to be here for all the final ends to be tied. Now she was off to Denver and the rest of our time together would be spent mostly through e-mail. Yay!

Alex was due at the house in a little less than two hours. I had to hurry if I was going to get dinner on the table by 6:00 pm. I was making chicken fettuccine Alfredo, steamed broccoli, and artisan bread. The pasta and bread were from scratch. If I learned anything from my mother, it was make it all yourself, it tastes better, it's cheaper, healthier and the satisfaction is wonderful. When Alex arrived, my house smelled seducing to a man's stomach. Perfect!

"Taryn, you look beautiful as always."

"Thank you." I was in a brightly colored halter top sundress and strappy sandals. Alex was wearing khaki-colored board shorts and a yellow polo. He looked good in every color I had seen him in. That's what happens when you have a dark color to your skin.

"Dinner smells great."

"Thank you, Alex." I started to grab the wine.

"Allow me." I felt his warm hand around my waist. "You worked hard to make this; you sit, I'll serve."

So I sat at the table and Alex brought out the wine and dished our plates. He already knew his way around my kitchen. I could get used to this. After dinner, he cleaned up the kitchen, telling me to sit and relax.

As he cleaned up we talked.

"What are some of your favorite things to do when you have free time?" I asked.

"I love hiking and camping. I like how it gets you away from the busy electronic world."

I agreed with him. "It's like it helps to reset your soul."

"Next time I'm in town we should try to plan a trip."

"That would be fun. I have all the gear we need too." When he was finished cleaning, we went for a walk. The summer air was warm. I held his strong hand, he felt so safe somehow. After our walk we returned home and stayed up watching movies again, kissing a little here and there, but this time I woke up in his arms.

Quickly, I felt myself under the covers I had my sleepshirt and underwear on. I was afraid to look at Alex his chest was bare; I started to pull up the covers to peek when he said.

"They're still on if that's what you're looking for."

"What!? I."

"Normally, I sleep in my birthday suit, but since we just met, I thought I'd keep the underwear on."

"Did we?" I didn't think I had that much to drink.

"No, you fell asleep on the couch, so I carried you in here. You look so cute when you sleep I thought I'd slip in next to you."

My cheeks flushed I knew my face was red. How could I not know if we had sex? I was such an idiot. I didn't know what to say, so I got up and went to the bathroom. When I came out, he was in the kitchen making coffee.

"So, um, did you sleep well?" What a stupid question. Agh!

"I did thank you, better than the couch, but next time I'll stay put."

"No! You don't have to, I mean, it was nice; the couch isn't that comfy, anyway." Ugh. I was so stupid.

We quickly fixed an egg and toast breakfast, he had to get out to the airport and get his plane ready for the trip home.

He pulled me close to him, kissing my neck and running his hands across my back. His warm lips brushed my cheek, moving to my lips. We kissed goodbye, and I wanted to cry. I was falling hard for him.

"I'll call you once I'm in Denver. I hope to come back in a couple of weeks maybe sooner."

"Okay, have a nice flight." Ugh. I closed the door and called Kandice.

"What is wrong with me? I don't date anyone after Robert and now I find the perfect guy and he doesn't even live here."

"Did you sleep with him?"

"No! But I did wake up in his arms! It felt so good."

"Taryn, you're 26 years old. It's okay to put out."

"He'll probably never call again."

"If he doesn't, he's not good enough for you. So is the rest of him hot?"

"Kandice!"

"What? I just want to know."

"Yes, every inch I could see, down to the boxer briefs, was hot. Dark olive skin and lots of smooth hard muscle."

"Nice. He'll call, stop worrying. I've gotta go, but I'll call ya later."

I could hear the door open. "Knock, Knock. I brought coffee."

I could have sworn I locked to the door when Alex left. Hmm.

"Robert, what do you want?"

"I brought you some coffee; I thought you might need it."

"Why?"

"Because I know your new guy had to leave town today." ▢

"How do you know that?"

"I spoke with him yesterday."

"What? Wait why?"

"You keep saying why a lot; you must need this coffee. Here just the way you like it, a hazelnut mocha without whipped cream. Now let's go to the patio and enjoy our coffee and then go for a run. That always makes you feel better."

"Robert, why are you here? Really?"

"Like I said before, I want to be your friend. If I can't have you as my wife, then can I at least have you as my friend?"

"Hmm." I eyed him suspiciously. I was still confused as to how he got in, but the coffee was nice, so I went out and sat with him. I did, however, get out of running with him. I told him I had just started my period, and the cramps were too bad to run. I'll probably have horrific cramps next cycle just for that lie, but it would be worth it to get him out of my hair. He hates to talk about things like that, it makes him uncomfortable. So it worked, and he left.

Chapter 5

The next few months went by pretty quickly. Alex and Marcy had come to Silver Springs every couple of weeks. Marcy seemed pleased with the progress but wasn't one to give much praise. The only way you knew you were doing a good job was if she hadn't accused you of screwing something up. As for Alex, we talked every day, and he stayed with me whenever he was in town. We had camped a few times on several of the mountain passes that surrounded Silver Springs.

Sadly, to Kandice's disappointment, we still have not slept together, but he does share my bed. He is closing on the condo in a couple of weeks. I can't wait until he has finally moved here. Robert has continued to annoy me all summer, sneaking into my place whenever he has a chance, and I'm still not sure if he follows me occasionally. At any rate, he's harmless, just annoying.

It was two weeks before the wedding. It was crunch time. I made sure Marcy had checked in at Crystal Lakes and that everything was okay. The only complaint she had was that the butler was weird, so I took it as things were perfect. Marcy's not happy unless she has something to complain about. Luckily for me, Marcy had half of her bridesmaids with her already, so I didn't have to keep her entertained; that was their job. Alex, I had just found out, was to be the best man at Marcy and Dan's wedding. We don't talk about our clients, and while I had suspected that Dan's company was one of Alex's clients, I'd never asked.

Alex and I were sitting on my patio enjoying a beautiful fall afternoon.

"Taryn, I need you to help me plan Dan's bachelor party. The girls are staying at a hotel Saturday night, one week before the wedding, so we could throw the party at Crystal Lake."

"I'm guessing you want an exotic dancer?"

"Well yes," he said, with a wide goofy smile across his face.

"Then we'll need to go to The Hidden Closet. I'll drive; let's go."

We got into my truck and drove to the only sex shop we had in town. It wasn't my first choice of places to take my new boyfriend. I guess you would call him "boyfriend" we really hadn't discussed our relationship. However, it was the only place in town where you could hire a private dancer. We walked into The Hidden Closet and wove our way through the lingerie racks to the checkout counter in the back.

"Taryn, how are you?" Asked Ella.

Ella is an ex-runway model for Victoria's Secret. She's about fifty-five years old, tall, blond, and dirty. She owns The Hidden Closet and is very willing to give you advice on any of your sexual needs. I love her.

"Fine, how's business?"

"Never better, sex sells. Ha. What can I do for you two? The toys are in the back room."

"Oh! Us! No!" I could feel my face getting red. "We are here to look through your exotic dancers' book. I'm planning a bachelor party."

"Okay, I have some new girls."

Ella doesn't hire these girls. However, she provides them with a way to get the job without advertising and giving their personal phone numbers out. Ella keeps a binder with photos and stage names. We pick the one or ones we like, and Ella contacts them, giving them my information. Then we set up a meeting with the girl and determine the price, expectations, and times. Once Ella contacts them, she has nothing else to do with it.

Alex looked through the book and picked a woman by the name of Bambi. She had dark brown hair, a tiny waist, and, of course, big boobs. She wore a lot of eye makeup, but beneath it, she was quite pretty. I let Ella know our choice, and she said she'd put in the call.

"Is there anything else I can do for you two?" Ella asked as she looked towards the room filled with sex toys.

Blushing and embarrassed, I shook my head no and grabbed Alex's hand, pulling him out of there. We got in the car, and Alex was grinning from ear to ear.

"What?"

"You go in there much?" He asked with a sly grin.

"No, yes, just for business, I plan a lot of parties. Don't say a word," I said as I pointed my finger at him. He made the lips-zipped signal as I pulled out of the parking lot. On the ride home, we planned the rest of the party. Bachelor parties are not hard to plan. You get a stripper, pick a theme, alcohol, and possibly party favors; then you're good to go.

I got a call from Bambi that afternoon; she could meet with us after 5:00 today. So we said we could meet her at 5:30, at The Old Irish Pub on Main St. I love The Old Irish Pub. There's a worn wooden bar and old wooden tables dispersed throughout. There is a stage for entertainers, and on Friday nights they have a band that plays just Irish music.

At 5:30, the thin brunette walked in. I could tell her boobs had to be fake, but that didn't stop every man's head from turning as she sauntered in. They bounced like giant water balloons and were spilling out of her tiny low-cut tank top. She walked right up to Alex and put her hand on his shoulder, not even making eye contact with me. I was sitting right next to him, for cripes' sake. My hand was on his knee; couldn't she see that we were together? I could feel my blood start to boil as she leaned into him, damn near sticking her boobs in his face. Oh, she'll be a good stripper. She had no problem throwing those babies around. I thrust my hand at her, pushing her back a bit.

"Hi, I'm Taryn. I'm the one you spoke to on the phone."

"Hi, I'm Bambi." The prissy-ass tone that came out of her made me want to choke her.

"Yeah, I know that! What do you charge?" I snipped.

"$75 an hour, unless you want to go topless, then it is $100."

"Yes, we'll go topless," Alex said.

My jaw dropped. I wanted to punch him.

"Good, lap dances are extra, so tell your boys to be prepared. I do a minimum of two hours, and I expect half that given to me at the door. I have several costumes: police, maid, or sailor, you name it, I can get it."

"Sailor," Alex said, way too eagerly.

I gave him an evil look. Disgusted, I let her know when and where she was to be. Then she turned and blew Alex a kiss goodbye and waved me off like yesterday's trash.

"I did not like her," I said to Alex after she left.

"I thought she was fine," he said, in that totally clueless way men can act.

My jaw dropped a second time, and a finger closed it. I looked up; it was Robert. "What are you doing here?" I said. At the same time, Alex was saying hi.

"You know him?"

"Yeah, we met a couple of months ago."

"Really?" I squinted my eyes and looked at Robert suspiciously. He blew the look off and sat down across from us.

"How do you two know each other?" Alex asked.

"Robert and I are uh... longtime friends," I said. "That's all!" I looked at Robert pleadingly. Not here, not now, please, I thought in my head. I'd tell Alex later about my history with Robert. He actually knew a little bit from our many conversations on the phone, but I hadn't gone through the whole agonizing story with him. We had only seen each other a few times over the summer, and I did not want to talk about that mess.

Somehow Robert weaseled his way into dinner with us and an invite to the bachelor party, which was just fantastic. I was still mad at that hooker we had hired and at Robert, so by the time we got home, I was ready for bed. Alex had decided to stay at Crystal Lakes tonight and asked me to join him, but with the mood I was in, it would not have been a good night. I declined, kissed him goodnight, and sent him on his way.

The rest of the week went by like a chaotic breeze. Alex and I spent very little time together since he was the pilot and best man. He was busy picking up family members and doing Dan's bidding. Not that I was any less busy, I had all the last-minute details to bring together and had to keep the bride as low stress as possible. So when the bachelor party rolled around, I didn't have time to think about how much I didn't like that floozy witch. I had, however, filled Kandice in on all of it. She was ready to camp out at the party and kick her ass, as always, for me. I told her there would be no ass-kicking, and even though I didn't like her, this still involved my job. Be professional, I told myself.

I arrived at Crystal Lake two hours before the party was supposed to start. I rang the doorbell, and Sam the butler answered. "Miss O'Kelly, please come in."

"Thank you, sir." He was a strange man, very polite, but weird, tall, deathly pale, and always in a hot suit. Alex was already here. Bambi was due in an hour and a half so she could get ready here before the party started.

I met Alex in the cinema room. We moved the furniture around to create a half-circle, hung decorations, and stocked the bar with items for the dirtiest named drinks and, of course, the old standby, beer. We placed a chair in the middle of the room for the trollop to dance on. The stereo, complete with surround sound, was in working order. She was going to bring her own music, but Alex had some of Dan's favorites too.

The doorbell rang, and I went out to see if it was her. Bambi came through the door and said a few things to Sam, but I couldn't hear them. He grabbed her arm; she jerked it away and pushed her way past him. Hmm, the creepy weird guy doesn't like big-boob whores either. I liked him more already.

I greeted Bambi with the most professional smile I could muster. "Hi, Bambi, ready for tonight?"

"Yeah, I make good money doing this-"

I cut her off before she could say anything else and showed her where she could get ready, then pointed her in the direction of the room she would be working in. I couldn't care less about what she had to say.

"I will let Alex know you are here. Once you are ready, meet us in the cinema room and he will give you your upfront fee."

"Alex? That hot guy I met the other day?"

"Yes, he is, and he's mine, so if I were you, I wouldn't try anything. I saw what you did the other day, and if I see it again, I might have to hurt you."

"Is that a threat?"

"You bet it is!" I growled at her. "Have a great show," I said in a sickeningly sweet, syrupy voice. Even I wanted to vomit when I heard that sound come out of me. I turned and walked away. My heart was racing. I had never done that before. Kandice would be so proud! I went back to Alex and said, "Your whore is here."

"She's not a whore; she's a dancer."

"Well, I can dance, but you don't see me putting my boobs in every man's face, especially one that clearly has someone with him." He heard nothing I said except...

"You can dance now I may have to see that sometime. What's your specialty?"

"The pole," I said in disgust. I had never danced provocatively in my life, but he didn't need to know that.

He leaned in and kissed me. "There is so much more I need to know about you. I don't want Bambi, I want you."

I turned to Jello once again in his arms. He continued to kiss me, then we heard a woman clear her voice. I turned to see Bambi. Ugh! Alex went over, talked to her, gave her some money, and sauntered back over to me.

"What are you doing next?"

"Going out with Kandice once the party is started."

"Stay here tonight with me in my room."

"I'm not staying for the party."

"No, come back and stay with me."

"It will be late."

"Hell, I'm only paying for a max of three hours; at her rates I'd be broke if it went any longer."

"I don't know."

"Tell you what; meet me in my room at 11:00; I'll be there even if the guys aren't done. If they want it to last longer, it will be on their pocketbooks."

"Maybe, if I'm still out I'll come by."

Once all the men had arrived, including Robert, I left. I met Kandice at Joe's sports bar. She was already waiting.

"Did it get started okay?"

"Yeah, but I wasn't very nice to the stripper. I kind of told her off. I was still mad."

"What did you say?"

"I basically told her I would hurt her if she touched Alex."

"I can't believe you; you must really like Mr. Hotpants."

"Stop calling him hotpants! He has a name; it's Alex, and yes, I really like him. You're rubbing off on me; I never should have threatened her. Alex wasn't going to do anything."

"Damn right I'm rubbing off on you, and it's a good thing too. You can't be nice to everyone; they'll walk all over you. She needed to know you exist. I'd have said more."

"How's Trey?" I asked, changing the subject. I didn't want to think about Bambi anymore. She put me in a grumpy mood.

"He's good, still as sexy as ever."

"It's been a few months now and you're not tired of him; he hasn't turned out to be a jerk?"

"Nope, he's out of town a lot, you know; I'm still not sure why exactly. He's very vague about his career."

"You don't think he's doing anything illegal, do you?"

"No, I think he's okay. He just doesn't like to talk about work. We spend our time together doing other things, if you know what I mean," she said as she raised her eyebrows and winked at me.

I rolled my eyes and shook my head.

We continued to talk for a couple of hours. It was 10 pm, and I had decided I was going to meet Alex. I wanted to be early to surprise him. I told Kandice I'd call her in the morning.

I went home to pack a few things and drove back out to Crystal Lakes; it was about 10:45 when I arrived. I thought I saw Robert on the deck talking to someone, but I couldn't see who. Something about getting the money. Whatever, I didn't really care. I just wanted to sneak up to Alex's room. If all went right, I might actually take Kandice's advice. I really wanted to; I think I can trust him; we had been dating for four months.

Sam let me in, and I ran up the stairs to Alex's room. I could hear laughter pouring out of the party room; I assumed it wasn't over yet. I put on a little silky black teddy that Kandice had gotten me as a get-over Robert present. I had never worn it. I thought, why not tonight? I turned off the lights, lit a candle, and sat in the chair, waiting for Alex. A little while later, I heard the door open and saw two shadows entering the room. I ducked behind the chair. It was the stripper. And who I assumed to be Alex. I started to cry and crept along the wall, trying to grab my things and sneak out. The whole time, I could hear them making out. Tears streamed down my face. I was trying to hold my breath so they couldn't hear me sobbing.

Once out of there, I wrapped myself in my robe and ran for the door. I ran as fast as I could to the truck. With snot and tears everywhere, I grabbed tissues and started to dry my face. Blowing my nose and took deep breaths to stop the crying. How could he do this to me? Why would he ask me to come back? Did he want me to see this? I climbed into my truck and started to pull away when something inside me said to wait. I wasn't going to take this, not again. I'm going back in there and kicking her ass. I stormed inside the house in a fit of rage, tears still streaming down my face. I threw open the door, slamming it behind me. Sam wasn't there to greet me. Which was probably a good thing. I stomped up the stairs. All I wanted was to break every bone in her body. I felt like I could kill her. I stormed up the stairs and pounded on the door.

"Alex!" I yelled, "Open up!" A door down the hall opened and Alex stepped out.

"Taryn, are you okay? What's going on?"

I quickly counted the doors down the hall. Had I banged on the wrong one? Robert opened the door in front of me.

"Hey baby, here to join the party?" He slurred.

What? He was drunk, very drunk. His breath reeked of alcohol. I had never seen him this drunk before. Then I heard Bambi call him back. I slapped Robert across the face and shoved him back in the room, closing the door, then turned to Alex, who now looked thoroughly confused.

"It's nearly midnight; you're late. Are you okay?" he asked as he came down the hall towards me.

"I thought you had decided not to come out."

"This is your room, right?"

"No, mine's the next one down."

"You didn't have that stripper with you earlier?"

"No, why?"

Great, now he's going to think I'm a jealous control freak.

"It's just that I snuck into your room to surprise you, and two people came in, and I thought that it was you and that stripper. So I left."

"But... then you came back?"

"Yeah, so I could... It wasn't you with her, was it?"

"No, I told you earlier I wanted you."

I started to cry again. He pulled me close and held me in his arms. Unfortunately, we spent the rest of the evening talking about what had really happened between Robert and me two years earlier. At least I don't think he thinks I'm crazy anymore.

"I need a drink, I'm going to the kitchen. I will be right back. Do you want anything?"

"No, I'm good," he said solemnly.

"Okay."

I hesitated a minute and went downstairs and could see light was slipping through the crack under the office door. I knocked on the door, but there was no answer. I opened the door, and no one was there. Hmm, Sam must have forgotten to turn the office light off. I switched it off and went to the kitchen. Fumbling in the dark, I grabbed a glass from the cabinet, flipped on the light, and screamed. There on the floor was Bambi, and she looked dead.

Chapter 6

The next few minutes seemed to take hours. Probably half the house heard me scream, but Alex and Robert were at my side first. Alex called 911, and Robert had managed to slip his arms around me without me realizing it. Alex was on the floor next to Bambi, checking for a pulse. I started to lay my head on Robert's shoulder, then realized what I was doing, I pulled away from him. He gripped me tightly, a little too tight; it hurt, and he didn't release until Alex put his hand on Robert's shoulder. I was a little weirded out by the awkward moment, but I grabbed Alex's hand and moved away from Robert and the body. Alex immediately started asking me questions.

"When you first noticed her, did you touch anything? Was she breathing when you found her?" My head started to spin. I felt like I was going to throw up. No, wait! I was going to throw up.

"Alex, I... I," put my hand to my mouth and ran for the bathroom. After a few minutes in the bathroom, I heard a knock.

"Taryn, the police are here. They need to talk to you. Can you come out?"

"Just a minute," I said. I washed my hands, rinsed my mouth out, and opened the door.

"This is Officer Ballenger, Taryn. He needs to speak with you."

I looked at Alex and back at Officer Ballenger.

"Okay," I said hesitantly.

Officer Ballenger was a short, stubby guy with a major receding hairline. But he had kind hazel-colored eyes framed with crow's feet. He stuck out his meaty hand and shook mine.

"Miss O'Kelly, I understand you're the one who found the body."

"Ya-yes, I am."

"What were you doing at the time in which you found the body?"

"I was getting a drink of water."

"What is your relationship with the victim?"

"I hired her to strip for the bachelor party," I said begrudgingly.

"I detect agitation in your voice? Would you care to elaborate?"

I explained the situation and all of the events leading up to the last time I saw Bambi alive. Trying to sound normal and not like a crazy jealous girlfriend. I felt like a little girl in trouble for getting out of bed. Being scolded for something I didn't do.

Officer Ballenger looked puzzled. "Did anyone else feel the way you felt about the victim?" he asked.

"I don't know? No one else appeared to have a problem with her, if that is what you are implying," I said. "But no one else is dating Alex either!"

After what felt like a very long interrogation with Officer Ballenger, Alex came over with another officer. The two officers talked for a minute before the new one approached me.

Alex introduced me to Detective David Parker.

"He is a friend of mine, the one who helped convince me to move here, that is, until I met you."

David Parker was an average-looking man with sandy-colored hair, a matching mustache, and cool, piercing blue eyes. I put out my hand.

"Nice to meet you, although I wish it could have been different circumstances."

"Me too," he said. "I know Officer Ballenger already asked you some questions, but I have a few more about the earlier events of the evening."

I went through the night's events in order from the setup of the party to the embarrassing mistaken room incident. That got what I think was a stifled smile, but I couldn't be sure. Great, now he'll probably tell Alex to run. I finished with what had happened in the kitchen.

He looked at me silently for a moment.

"Did anyone hear what you told the victim about you and Alex?"

"I don't think so. I didn't do anything to her. I was mad; she practically smashed her boobs into Alex's face."

I could see Alex from the corner of my eye; I couldn't tell if he was upset. I hadn't told him about my threat to Bambi. I guess I can kiss this one goodbye too. All thanks to another stripper. Agh.

"Detective Parker, I've told you everything; every embarrassing detail. Please, may I go now?" He looked over at Alex and motioned for him to come over.

"She can go for now, but I will be in contact."

He pulled Alex aside and whispered something to him. I saw Alex nod and turn to come back to me. He didn't look happy.

"Right now, he has you threatening her, and Robert looks to be the last one seen with her alive. Why did you threaten her?"

"Because I didn't like how she threw herself at you in the pub, especially with me sitting right next to you. It was rude and slutty. Then when she came in, she was talking about how hot you were. I just wanted her to keep her dirty hands off of you." That got a chuckle out of him. His eyes softened, and he pulled me close.

"The time of death will clear you; you were with me the whole time after we saw her with Robert." He kissed me. "You can trust me."

"Robert! I had completely forgotten about him. You don't think he did it, do you? I mean, I know he likes sex, but she seemed quite willing."

"I don't know, but the police will figure it out."

I leaned into Alex. "Can I go home? I'm tired."

"I'll check with David and then I'll drive you home."

The house was swarming with police looking for clues. Bambi had been strangled, and someone in that house had to have done it. On the drive home I was quiet, thinking about what had happened, but more selfishly, why I had let myself turn into a jealous green-eyed monster. I wished I hadn't said anything to her. I wished I hadn't come back. Alex was quiet on the drive too. I wondered what he was thinking.

Could Robert really have done it? He had gripped me hard, so hard it hurt when I had wanted to leave. He had been acting strangely over the last few months, showing up everywhere, knowing everything I was doing. That didn't add up as to why he would kill a stripper. As a matter of fact, if he wanted me back so badly, why had he slept with her in the first place? He said he had changed. Nothing he's done has made sense. No, he couldn't be a murderer; a cheating pig, yes, but a murderer, no. I must have looked very frustrated because Alex touched my leg. I jumped.

"Are you going to be okay?"

"What? Yes. I was just thinking. None of this adds up."

"Don't worry about it; let the police worry. You need to get some rest. I can't stay, but I'll be by later, okay?"

"Why can't you stay?"

"David asked me to come by the station."

"Is everything okay?"

"I am sure everything will be just fine."

We pulled up to my house; it was four in the morning. He opened the car door for me and walked me up the steps. After he made sure I was settled in, he leaned in and kissed me long and hard.

"I like the black thing," he whispered into my ear. "Maybe next time, I'll actually get to enjoy you in it."

With that, he turned and left. I locked the door and went straight to bed.

I woke up to the smell of coffee brewing. Mmm. Alex came back. I went into the kitchen to find Robert making coffee instead of Alex.

"What are you doing, Robert? How did you get in?" I screeched at him!

"Shhh, don't yell. I needed to talk to you." Robert said quietly.

He had sunglasses on. He was hungover and had a migraine.

"You could have called."

"No, I needed to see you. Last night meant nothing to me. She seduced me."

"No, Robert, you have a problem with self-control."

"I was drunk."

"Yes, you were very drunk, and I don't care if you slept with her. I really don't. It's your business. That's the beauty of not being with you. You can do whatever you want, and I don't have to deal with it."

"Then why did you slap me last night?" He asked, befuddled.

"Because you called me baby and wanted me to join your little sex party. Robert, please go . I have a lot of work to do. Thanks for the coffee, but go." I pointed towards the door.

He started to walk away, turned back around, grabbed me, and kissed me. I pulled away, and he let me go.

"Sorry, Taryn, I really am," he said as he left.

I had hoped last night was just a horrible dream. I had fires to put out and quick. I called Alex's cell to see if he knew anything and got his voicemail.

"Hi, Alex, it's Taryn. I was just wondering if you had heard anything. I need to talk to Dan and Marcy about the wedding. Please call me as soon as you get this." I called Kandice; she said she'd be right over. I needed to call my mom, but it was Sunday. She would be at Mass, wondering why I wasn't at Mass, plus I didn't want to talk to her until I had more to tell her.

I heard a knock followed by, "Taryn, I'm here."

"Kandice, I'm so glad you could come over." She sat quietly as I told her the whole story.

"Well, kudos to you, Taryn, for going back in and confronting him, but are you sure you were ever in the wrong room, and where was everyone else when you were pounding on the door? Had they all left the party? Where was the weird butler?"

"I asked Alex if I had the right room, and he said that his room was the next one down. I'm sure I was in the room I pounded on, though."

"Tell me again what happened after you left me at Joe's. Try to remember every detail."

I started through the story again. "I came here first and packed a small overnight bag, then got in the truck and drove out to Crystal Lakes. Once there, I thought I saw Robert on the deck talking to someone, but I couldn't see who."

"Did you hear anything he or the other person said?"

"I don't think so. Wait, he did say something about needing the money tonight."

"Why would he need money?"

"Maybe it wasn't for him."

"What happened next?"

"I rang the bell and Sam opened the door. He greeted me like always."

"What did he say to you?"

"Good evening Miss O'Kelly, back again?" I did my best weird butler impression.

"Yes, I'm here to surprise Alex."

"You know where his room is right?" I said, still impersonating Sam.

"Yes, top of the stairs to the left."

"That's correct. Good Night."

"I replied goodnight. He went back into the office and I ran up the stairs."

"So you even checked where the room was and still somehow ended up in the wrong one?" Kandice replied. "Interesting, go on."

"Like I said before, I could hear laughter coming from the party. I went into the room, changed in the bathroom, freshened up my make-up and hair, and turned off the lights. I left a single candle glowing on the dresser and sat in the chair waiting."

"How long did you wait?"

"I don't know 10-15 minutes. Then, who I assumed to be Alex but was really, Robert, and that stripper came into the room. They were only making sex sounds, not talking."

"Fun. I'm not one for listening," Kandice raised her eyebrows.

"I ran out to the truck and started to drive away but decided to confront him. I turned around and re-parked. I was so mad I slammed my door and stormed back into the house. Sam wasn't around when I let myself in. The house was quiet, I stomped up the stairs, and you know the rest. The house was dark when I went into the kitchen."

"Alex never left your side while you guys had your talk?"

"No, we sat on the bed and I went over the whole story of Robert and me. I told him what I saw in the room and how I thought it was him. After that, he held me a while and said he was sorry I had to go through all that. Then I needed a drink. I got up, went to the bathroom, and on down to the kitchen."

"Where were Dan and the other grooms-men?"

"They were upstairs asleep, I guess. When I came out of the bathroom, everyone was up. I saw Dan, Ryan, and Jason all sitting in the foyer awaiting their interviews. Ryan and Jason are the other two groomsmen."

"So here is what we have so far: Robert talking to someone about money and sleeping with Bambi. You threatening Bambi, somehow ending up in the wrong room, and watching your ex sleep with her. You also mentioned that you didn't think Sam liked Bambi either."

"Yes, but that was just because of the way she had entered the house. Let me call Alex again." I said, as I pulled my phone out. I wondered why he hadn't called me back.

"Yeah, see what he knows about Dan and the groomsmen."

I called Alex again and still no answer so I left another message.

"Why hasn't he called to check on you?" Kandice was getting annoyed.

"I don't know, but I could call Marcy and try to talk to Dan."

"Yes, let's do that," Kandice said sarcastically. "Are you crazy? You do not want to talk to her; she'll never let you go. She'll go on a rant about the wedding being ruined. Avoid her for the time being."

"Okay, then what should we do?"

"Plan B, let's go out to Crystal Lakes."

"No, let's not," I said, "I don't want to go back there."

"Don't you want to know what really happened?"

"Not really," I said, "I would like to pretend that none of this happened."

"Well, I'm going out there without you then."

"Fine," I groaned, "I will go with you." I got dressed in jeans and a sexy low-cut top, scrunched my hair, and swiped on some mascara. The mascara was for nothing because no amount of makeup could hide the dark circles under my swollen, puffy, red eyes. I grabbed my gun, and we piled into Kandice's Jeep Wrangler.

"What are we going to do when we get out there?" I asked.

"Root around, that's what!" Kandice said

We drove into the circular driveway and parked right out front. We went up to the door and rang the bell. To my surprise, Mrs. Williams answered the door.

"Hello Miss O'Kelly, come in, dear. What can I do for you?"

"I am here to see how the investigation is going and hopefully talk to some of the wedding party."

"Ah yes, terrible thing happening to that poor girl. The police left a short while ago."

"Where's Sam?"

"He took the day off, up all night, you know." She looked past me to Kandice.

"Oh, I'm sorry. This is my friend Kandice."

"Nice to meet you, dear."

She let us in and went back into the office. The first thing I wanted to do was look in the rooms. Kandice and I went up the stairs to the left, and I knocked on the first door no answer. We turned the knob and went in. The bed was a mess and the candle I had lit was still sitting on the dresser.

"Look Kandice! This is the room I was in. That's where I put the candle." We searched the room and didn't find anything else of interest so we left and went down the hall to the next room.

"This is Alex's real room," I told Kandice. We knocked. No answer. So we went in. We looked around the room. It was just like we had left it last night. Nothing had been touched, not that I could tell anyway. Alex must not have come back up here last night. As we were about to leave, I noticed something on the floor behind the little chair. A tube of lipstick, and it wasn't mine. I rolled it up; it was bright red, the same color Bambi had on last night. I also found a crumpled-up piece of paper under the bed. I uncrumpled it; all it had on it was the initials J.S. 303-. It looked like someone had started to write more but for some reason, didn't finish. Before we could investigate further, we heard a knock at the door. Kandice and I ducked under the bed.

"Alex, you in there?" The door opened; someone walked in. All we could see were feet. The shoes were black leather, sort of pointy-toed. The man walked around the room. It sounded like he was rifling through stuff, looking for something. After a couple of minutes of searching, he left.

Kandice and I didn't want to get caught; we shimmied out from under the bed and high-tailed it out of there. We went to Ryan's and Jason's room and knocked, no answer.

"They all must be out." I said.

"I don't blame them after what happened last night."

"Kandice, can you get Dan's cell number? I wouldn't have to call Marcy then."

Kandice called her Aunt Mia and got Dan's cell.

"Awesome, let's call him now and see if the guys will meet us somewhere. You call Dan, that way maybe Marcy won't know what's going on."

"Dan, hi, it's Kandice. I need to meet you and your groomsmen if possible. How about my place? Okay, see in about a half-hour."

"They're all coming except Alex, he's not with them right now."

"Where are they? Did he say where Alex was?"

"At the hotel with the girls. He didn't say where Alex is."

"Let's get going."

As we were going down the stairs, Mrs. Williams appeared from nowhere to greet us. I jumped and squealed!

"Sorry Mrs. Williams you startled me. Did Alex or anyone else come by since we got here?"

"Sam did, but only for a minute, he had something to pick up."

"Did you know the wedding party isn't here? I knocked on all their doors, but no one answered."

"Oh, they must have left before I got here to take over for Sam."

"Have a nice day Mrs. Williams," I said as we left.

"You too, dear."

"She's lying," Kandice said, as we drove away. "She knew the guys weren't here all along."

"Then why would she let us in?"

"I don't know yet, but she's on my list of suspicious people, anyway."

"I'm more concerned about who owns those pointy black shoes and why he was in Alex's room."

"What do you know about this Mrs. Williams?"

"She's the property manager; she's not there every day unless the renters request she be their cook. Dan and Marcy did not, it's extra, and they didn't feel they needed it. She comes in to clean about once a week."

"What about Sam?"

"He's there almost every day and honestly, I don't know what else he does besides answer the door and sit in the office. There is a servant's cottage somewhere on the property, but I haven't seen it. I think he lives there. When we booked the place, we only dealt with Mrs. Williams."

We drove the rest of the way in silence, lost in our own thoughts.

Chapter 7

Silver Springs has mountains surrounding the town with a road following the river through it. Kandice's house backs up against one of the mountains. It's a wildlife preserve with hiking trails all over it. Her backyard is a forest. The house is a 1950s stick-built with a cute little porch; it even has a two-seater porch swing. The lot is small, but it is completely fenced, which is nice for her little dog Fluffy. He is a Shetland sheepdog, super friendly, and very cute. As we came through the gate, Fluffy bounded out to greet us. We decided to wait on the porch for the boys to show up.

As the guys pulled up to the house, my stomach turned a little. I didn't even know Ryan and Jason and I was going to ask them what happened with the stripper last night.

"Hi, guys!" We waved as they walked up.

"How's Marcy doing?" I asked Dan.

"She's hysterical, she hates the stripper, she's mad at Alex for getting one, and needs to talk to you."

"Well, that's why Kandice called you guys. I need to get some more information, then I'll call Marcy and get the whole thing straightened out. Dan, you go first. Tell me everything you can remember from last night, every detail."

"When I got to the party, everyone was already there except for the stripper; she was still getting ready. There were ten of us. Alex, Ryan, Jason, Robert, myself, and a few guys I went to school with. They all told the usual old ball and chain jokes and teased me about marriage. Bambi came out and performed. There was a lot of alcohol and loud music from that point on. I didn't pay for any of her lap dances, but she gave me one for free just for being the groom. I didn't ask for it. Everyone else paid for one or two except Robert; he paid for several. We all decided she liked Alex in particular because she was on him every free chance she got."

"What! After I told her..." Kandice grabbed my arm to stop me. I could feel my blood starting to boil.

"Go on," she said.

"Alex never paid her anything that I saw, and he always put his hand up as to show he wasn't doing anything. He really wasn't that interested in her. None of us were. It was just good fun."

That cooled me off a bit.

"Robert left before the show was over, and I didn't see him again. Alex left with the stripper to pay her the rest of her fee, and the guys and I hung out a little longer. By the time Alex got back, everyone was leaving."

"What did you do after?"

"Alex, Ryan, Jason, and I all talked a little but quickly dispersed and headed for bed. Alex told me that the stripper followed him up to his room and nearly begged him to sleep with her, but when he refused, she slapped him and left. I know the reason he refused; it's because he loves you and wouldn't do anything to screw up any chance he might have with you."

He loves me, I thought! Now I felt all mushy inside; he really didn't want her.

"I went upstairs and had a message from Marcy saying if I was still up I could call her. So I called her and talked for a good hour or more before falling asleep. I thought I heard a scream, but I was still groggy and a little drunk, so I wasn't sure if I was just dreaming. When I heard the sirens, I scrambled out of bed, knowing it wasn't a dream. Once downstairs, I found what you had already discovered, Bambi dead on the kitchen floor. Not the best way to end a bachelor party."

"No, it isn't. Last night was a horrible night. Ryan, you're up. Tell me what you remember about last night."

"Like Dan said, we were all swapping stories until she arrived. Then, that stripper came out and did some of the dirtiest dancing I've ever seen. She was well worth the money. The show was good, and she did have a thing for Alex, man, she was grinding on him."

"Ya, ya, I heard that already," I growled with annoyance. Kandice grabbed my arm again; this time it hurt.

"Ouch!" I glared at her. Ryan looked uncomfortable.

"Um, sorry, uh, go on," I said, trying to sound comforting.

"Well, Robert didn't look too well, so he went outside. Shortly after he left, Bambi finished and went with Alex to collect the rest of her money. Alex did come back with one bright red cheek. Once everyone was gone, Jason and I went upstairs to edit the video."

"What video?"

"Oh yeah, me and Jason secretly videoed the whole show, but the police have it now."

Damn, I wanted to see it, I thought to myself.

"When we were done, we went to bed. I didn't hear your scream; I think I was passed out."

"Okay, Jason, what do you have to add?"

"Not much, Taryn, you heard Dan and Ryan. That's pretty much how I remember it. I agree with Ryan about Robert; he didn't look so well. I think he was sick. I didn't see him again until the police were there. I walked the other guys from school out, so I know they left. Alex's face was red, and Ryan and I did go up to edit the movie, but like he said, the PD took it."

"Did you see anyone else when you walked the guys out?"

"No the office light was on with the door closed, so I assume Sam was still there."

"Okay, guys, thanks. Dan, please tell Marcy I'm working on it and I will call as soon as possible. You should take her to the hot springs; it might take her mind off things."

"Great idea, Taryn. Thanks," Dan said, with a grateful nod.

"Bye, guys," we waved as they drove away.

"Those dirty boys. I can't believe they video-taped the whole show. Maybe I don't want to strip after all. The last thing I want is to end up on YouTube."

"That's the last thing you want? Gosh, I thought it would be the dirty men trying to grab at you or saving your video for later."

"No, those people watching YouTube would get it for free."

"Kandice! You're awful!"

"Ha, ha. Just kidding, mostly. I don't want to be in anyone's movie, thanks."

"So now we know why her lipstick was in his room," I said. "That horrible woman followed him up there after I told her hands off, but how'd she end up with Robert?"

"We'll just have to find out," Kandice said, grinning.

My phone rang finally; it was Alex. "Hi Alex, what's up?"

"Sorry, I haven't called you back. I've been very busy. How are you doing today?"

"Okay, I suppose. What about you?"

What I really wanted to say was, after a night like last night, how do you think I feel? Then you just abandon me, what the hell? Some great protective boyfriend you are. But I thought better of it.

"Just fine," he said, sounding a little annoyed.

"Can I see you?"

"Yeah, meet me at your place in an hour," he said.

"Okay."

"Kandice, that was Alex. I need to meet him at my place, but I want to be alone with him. I don't want him thinking I am getting myself into trouble."

"I would rather you be alone with him for other reasons, but I'll drop you off. I have some errands to run before work tomorrow, anyway. But I want to know what happens."

"Actually, do you mind taking me to get my truck?"

"Sure, that works for me."

"Thanks, Kandice, and of course I will call you the second I get a chance and fill you in."

Once at Crystal Lakes, I jumped out of the Jeep. Waving goodbye to Kandice, I climbed into my truck and headed home.

Alex was waiting on the steps, looking particularly delicious in snug-fitting jeans and a blue T-shirt when I pulled up.

"So what have you been up to today?" He asked.

"Trying to figure out what exactly happened last night, so I can move forward with Dan and Marcy's wedding. What about you?"

"I was talking to the police. Trying to clear you," he said flatly.

"Me! I'm not wanted." My voice was high-pitched and screechy. Yeesh, that sounded wonderful.

"You're on their list of suspects."

"What! Why, because I told her to leave you alone?"

"People have killed for a lot less, Taryn."

I rolled my eyes in disgust and groaned. "Ugh... What do you know so far?"

"Not a lot. She was strangled with what looks to be the wire from a meat thermometer. They found the wire under the cabinet next to her body. Your alibi is probably the strongest because you were with me, but your threat certainly doesn't help. All the other guys claim they were asleep. Sam has said that no one else but you showed up last night. After the party ended, half the group left almost immediately, leaving very few of us in the house."

"What does the video show?"

"How do you know about that?"

"I've talked to all the wedding party except you today. You wouldn't return my phone calls, so I did a little investigative work myself. I also know that she was in your room with you last night; I found her lipstick beside your chair." His face hardened; he did not look happy.

"Taryn, you don't know what you're doing."

"Alex, you said she wasn't in your room. Did I see you, or was it Robert kissing her last night? I know she followed you to your room. I know she slapped you when you turned her down."

"It wasn't me," he growled. "She threw herself at me. She did kiss me, but I stopped it. She slapped me, took her money, and stormed out. That was the last time I saw her alive."

"Why didn't you tell me last night? I poured my soul out to you."

"You were so upset. Why would I tell you that the stripper you hate kissed me and tried to make more out of it? I told you nothing happened, and nothing did. Taryn, it bothers me to know that someone in the house killed her, that the killer knows us, and is still out there. Please just leave the investigation to the police."

I gave a halfhearted shrug.

He grabbed me by the shoulders and shook me gently. "Taryn, promise me."

"I promise," I said with my fingers and toes crossed.

"Would you want to come to dinner at my mom's tonight? She would like to meet you, and since it's Sunday, I know dinner will consist of something to do with mashed potatoes, and the dessert will be a pie of some sort. I'll warn you now. My family can be a little crazy, sometimes embarrassing, but usually fun," I said, trying to change the subject to something lighter.

"I would love to meet your mother. If she's anything like you, I like her already." He tapped his finger on the end of my nose.

We went into the house and called my mother. "Hi, Mom, it's Taryn."

"Taryn, I didn't see you at Mass today. Is everything alright?" She asked worriedly.

"Yes, Mom, I wasn't feeling well, but now I'm better." Oh, please, God, forgive me for that lie. I didn't want to tell her about the murder just yet. "I wanted to let you know I'm bringing Alex to dinner tonight." I think I heard a quiet squeal on the other end of the phone, but I wasn't sure. "It's okay, right?

"Yes, yes, of course, dear. I've been waiting to meet him for some time now. Does this mean grandchildren potential?"

"Not sure yet, but possibly."

"Yay! Dinner's at 4:00 today, same as every Sunday."

"Love you, Mom, bye."

I sat down on the couch next to Alex and let him know dinner was at 4:00. I laid my head on his shoulder, and before I knew it, I was asleep. When I woke up, Alex was on the patio talking on his cell. I wanted to eavesdrop, but before I could get close enough to hear, he ended the call.

"You're awake," he said as he walked through the door. "It's 3:30. Are you ready to go to your mom's?"

"I slept a long time," I said as I yawned and stretched.

"You needed it."

"I guess," I yawned again. "Let me run to the restroom, and then we can go." I brushed my hair and teeth, touched up my mascara, and was ready to go.

Alex grabbed my waist and pulled me in for a kiss with a lot of tongue. "Have I told you how hot you are? Maybe we should skip dinner and go right to dessert." He kissed me again.

"It would be fun except I already called my mom, and she would be very upset if we don't show up."

Damn it! Why do I always feel like I need to do the right thing? Because I am a good girl, I told myself. "Let's go before I change my mind."

"Can, I change your mind?" he asked, with a sly grin on his face.

"No! Come on." I grabbed his hand and dragged him out the door.

We walked up the steps to my mother's house. Should I have brought him with me? Maybe this was a bad idea? Was I ready for him to meet my family? My family was intense, and that was an understatement. And what about last night? The events still were a puzzle to me, and I wasn't sure how Alex's piece fit. Too late now. Scotty answered the door before we even knocked.

"Hi, Taryn!" He turned and looked Alex over. I guess he approved because he put out his hand. "I'm Scotty, Taryn's brother. Nice to meet you," he said as they shook hands.

Scotty can come off as a bit hostile if he's not sure of someone, particularly anyone I hang out with. We followed Scotty into the house, where he proceeded to announce that we were here. I leaned over and whispered to Alex not to mention last night's events.

"I won't if you don't," he whispered back.

My mother came running. "Alexander," she gushed, "so nice to finally meet you. I'm Molly, Taryn's mother."

"Nice to meet you too, Mrs. O'Kelly," Alex replied.

My dad came in. "So, do you like guns, Alex?"

"Yes, sir, I always carry one."

"Good, so you could protect my daughter should she need it? Although she handles one pretty good herself. Isn't that right, Taryn?"

"Yes, Dad." He has always tried to scare away the guys I've brought home with his gun talk.

"Scotty and I competition shoot, you should join us sometime," my dad suggested, eyeing Alex.

"I would love to, Mr. O'Kelly." Alex chuckled in return.

"Call me Bill. So, Alex, what are your intentions with my daughter? You have been dating a little while now?"

"Not now, Dad."

I grabbed Alex's hand and pulled him over to his seat at the table. Alex looked back at my dad and said, "Only good things Bill, she is an amazing woman."

"I'm glad you think so. She is."

We sat down for dinner, and like I said, it was mashed potatoes and gravy. This time it accompanied a pot roast. This time it accompanied a pot roast.

"Well, aren't you a handsome man," Gramma said as she sat down next to Alex.

I blushed. Alex didn't even blink an eye; he just said thank you. I figure it's because he knew how good he looked.

"Alex, this is my grandma. Gramma this is Alex." I knew that my gramma would size Alex up before anyone else with her special talents, and I was not fearful of what she would think. I just hoped that maybe someday I would get her special powers.

"Alex, the eyes are a window to the soul. Your eyes are dark, warm, and inviting. I believe you do only intend good things for my granddaughter. Your soul is old; she could learn from you."

"Okay, Gramma, no more voodoo tonight." I didn't think she would tell Alex what she thought. I figured she would just tell me later. This is shaping up to be a great night. If he doesn't run away screaming by the time dinner is done, I might actually have a keeper. Ugh... I crossed my fingers.

The clanking of plates filled the air as we passed around the meal.

"Alex, Taryn tells me you're a pilot," my dad said as he shoveled a piece of pot roast dipped in mashed potatoes into his mouth.

"Yes, I am. I fly for private companies."

"Where'd you get your pilot's license?"

"It was during my time in the Air Force."

"You served this great country; I like that in a young man. I served in the Marines and Scotty here in the Army," my dad said as he squeezed my brother's shoulder.

"Taryn said you are moving here," my mother said.

"Yes, I close on my condo very soon. It's just down the street from Taryn's. Actually, she is the one that showed it to me the first day we met," he said, giving me a smile.

"How is that going to work with your job?" My father asked.

"It should be fine since most of my clients have planned trips; rarely is it a last-minute thing, and even if it is, I usually have enough time to get from here to Denver, anyway."

The rest of dinner was about the same, my family interrogating Alex and my dad talking about the military. It was chilly outside when we left my parents, and I was drained. It had been a long day.

"Your family's fun," Alex said once we were in the car.

"They didn't scare you with all their questions?" I asked.

"No, clearly they love you and wanted to check me out."

"Thanks for not saying anything about the murder."

"They'll find out tomorrow; it will be in the paper."

"I know, and I'm not sure how to handle that. To quote Scarlet O'Hara, 'I won't think about that today; I'll think about it tomorrow. After all, tomorrow is another day.'"

Alex laughed a warm laugh, and it made me feel all gooey inside. He put his hand on my thigh, which didn't help with the gooey feelings.

"I'll go talk to them tomorrow. I've got to meet David first thing, and then I'll go see your parents. Hopefully, by then you'll be off their list."

We pulled up to my house and walked up the steps: the night had turned bitterly cold, so we started the pellet stove and snuggled up together in front of it. Alex's cell phone rang, and he went to the bedroom to take the call. I sat in front of the fire in a daze, thinking about the events in the last twenty-four hours. Who had killed Bambi and why? I was deep in thought when Alex came up behind me, I jumped, startled.

"I didn't mean to scare you."

"You didn't. I just didn't hear you come up behind me."

"Taryn, I've got to go. I might be back later, but if it gets too late, I'll stay at a hotel. I don't want to wake you, and I don't want you to leave the door unlocked."

"I'll just give you my spare key. I want you to come back tonight. Where are you going?" I asked, standing up and piling the blanket on the couch.

"Business, I'm sorry I can't discuss it," he said reluctantly.

"Oh, okay." I went to the front entryway to retrieve my spare key only to find it was missing. "That's funny; it's not here."

"Could you have put it somewhere else? When's the last time you used it?" Alex asked.

"No, I always put it on the hook with my other keys, that way it doesn't get lost. The last time I used it was months ago. I had Scotty come to check on Giselle while I was away."

"Maybe you never got it back from him?" He suggested.

"I suppose. I guess I'll give him a call and see. Here, just take mine. You'll be back before I have to go anywhere. Besides, Kandice has a key. If I need to leave, I can always call her." I hesitated for a moment. "Alex, do you really have to go tonight? Can't this business wait? It's cold and late."

He didn't argue with me. Instead, he smiled softly and began to sing *"Baby, It's Cold Outside,"* his voice low and warm.

I joined him without thinking, slipping into the other part as naturally as breathing.

We got through a good chunk of the song and laughed. Then he leaned in and put his hand on my waist. I instantly warmed; he smelled so good. His breath was warm against my neck. I melted into his arms, and he kissed me. There was just a small slip of his tongue; then he pulled away.

"That's one of my favorite songs," I whispered.

"Mine too," he said. He turned and walked out into the cold night. I closed the door behind him, leaning back against it with a heavy sigh.

Chapter 8

I woke suddenly, around 1:00 AM, feeling as though someone was staring at me. A little creeped out, I flipped the light switch on and quickly scanned the room. No staring eyes watching me. I got up, grabbed my gun, and peeked outside my room. Nothing. As I crept down the hallway with my gun drawn, I switched on the rest of the lights in the house. No one was there. Since when had I become so paranoid? Giselle opened one eye at a half squint, closed it again, she wrapped her paw around her face. Clearly, I had been wrong and was disturbing her sleep, but I couldn't shake the feeling that something wasn't right. Where was Alex? What kind of meeting lasts past one in the morning? A slight breeze brushed across me. It felt like it was coming from my patio door. I froze. I knew I hadn't left the patio door open, not on a cold night like this. My patio door was cracked slightly; there on my dining room table stood an upright tube of lipstick.

Chills ran through my body. I kept my gun drawn and slowly walked towards the open door. Grabbing the handle with one hand and my gun aimed straight with the other, I swiftly slid the door shut and locked it. I couldn't see anyone on the patio.

I did a thorough check of my entire place, including behind the shower curtain, the whole time ready to shoot at whatever monster was willing to jump out at me. I found nothing. No one was here. I picked up the lipstick and rolled it up. It was the same bright red that Bambi had on. I heard a knock at the door and I nearly jumped out of my skin, dropping the lipstick. Terrified to answer, I ran to my office window to see who it was. Robert?

I opened the door. There stood a very drunk Robert.

"Hey baby," he slurred, "I was in the neighborhood and saw your lights on, so I thought I'd come up."

"Why?"

"I dunno, just to check on you. To see how you're doing. Why do you have your gun? Is everything okay?"

I looked down at the gun in my hand.

"Oh, I..." Tears started to well up behind my eyes. I was not going to cry, especially not to Robert. I blinked really fast and took a couple of deep breaths. Then, because I must be crazy, I let him in and told him what had happened. I had never seen a man sober up so fast.

After a few minutes, he got up and checked the whole house out. It felt a little weird having him look over the place. We hadn't been together here. This was my Robert-free memory zone, and yet it felt good in a strange way. I yawned; it was way too late, or too early, to be up. I asked Robert to go so I could go back to bed. I felt a little better now that we had checked all the door and window locks, and I felt pretty safe, besides I hoped Alex would be home soon.

"No, Taryn, I'm staying the night. I don't want whoever was here to come back and you to be alone."

"I won't be," I said. "Alex should be home soon."

He stiffened at the sound of that.

"So he has moved in, has he?"

"No, he's staying here until his place is ready, not that it's any of your business. Besides, I thought you two were great friends now."

"I like the guy..."

I raised a questioning eyebrow.

"I really do, but he's just not the right guy for you."

"And what, you are?" I snapped. "Please, Robert, spare me the I've changed speech. I can't go through it with you again."

"I wasn't going to do that to you again. It's just that something feels off about him."

"That's funny, I think he feels the same way about you," I said with a scowl.

"Why isn't he here to protect you? Why is he off in the middle of the night? He should be here checking over the place if he gets to share your bed," Robert pointed out.

I was dumbfounded. Bed-sharing in the sense he had meant hadn't actually happened, but I hadn't expected that from him. Sadly, I sort of felt the same way, but I wasn't about to let him know that.

"I'm staying," he said, crossing his arms.

"Fine! If you're going to stay, you can have the couch. When Alex comes home, I don't want to hear a word about where he sleeps." He made the lips-zipped signal, and I threw a pillow at him, smacking him in the face.

With Robert neatly tucked away and the pending awkwardness of having two sexy men in my house at once. I went to bed, but not for long. I could hear the fumbling of keys at the front door. Alex was finally home. He slid into bed; I could smell alcohol on his breath. He was very friendly, but I pretended to be asleep. Believe me, it was hard to do. My body was giving me confusing signals. I wanted him, but I could feel my blood starting to boil, but why? He had every right to be out. I didn't own him. We had barely been dating, but the things that Robert had said came back. Why had he left me? If he was that worried about me, he could have gotten home sooner. I fell asleep with all those disturbing thoughts swirling through my brain.

Wake-up time came too soon. Rolling over, I found that Alex was already out of bed. Ah! Robert was still on the couch! This is going to be a great day. I felt just as cranky as I had been when I went to sleep. I grabbed my robe as I flew out of the bedroom and hurried down the hall. Slowing to a walk, I saw the guys sitting at the table, drinking coffee and discussing lipstick.

"Good morning," they said in unison.

Okay, this is weirder than I thought it would be, my ex and my boyfriend chatting over coffee, sitting at my table, and acting normal.

"Good morning," I said hesitantly.

"Taryn, we need to talk about the lipstick. Why didn't you call me?" Alex asked.

"Why didn't I call you?" I shouted. "Well, let's see, it was one in the morning, and your business meeting was obviously running late. Luckily, Robert showed up just after it happened."

Why was I so upset with Alex? Why hadn't I called him last night, even if Robert was here? Out of the corner of my eye, I could see Robert. He had a stupid grin on his face.

"And you! Wipe that stupid grin off your face. What in the world were you doing outside my place so early in the morning anyway?" I wanted to cry, but I was too angry. Both of them sat there staring at me and looking confused by my outburst.

"It's the two of you that need to explain to me what's going on! Why do I have that stripper's lipstick on my table?"

I huffed to the kitchen to get a cup of much-needed coffee, only to find the pot was empty. Those jerks! I spun around, stormed out of the kitchen, and went to my room. I slammed the door and quickly got dressed. I grabbed my purse and cell and decided to walk to Penny's coffee house. I needed a fancy coffee now anyway.

"Taryn, wait." I could hear them both call.

"No! I need coffee, and I need it now! If the two of you want to talk to me, I'll be back when I get my coffee." With that, I stormed off.

I punched Kandice's number into my phone while I walked to the coffee shop.

"Hey! Kandice, I'm going to the coffee shop. I need you to meet me. Last night someone broke into my house and left Bambi's lipstick on my table. Robert came by, drunk, and stayed over. Alex was at a meeting and didn't get home until sometime after two. There's not much else to tell, but could you meet me?"

"On my way. You had both of them stay at your house last night?" Kandice shouted through the phone.

"Well, it's not as bad as it sounds, if Alex had been home Robert wouldn't have stayed. Hey, I'm at the shop we can talk about this when you get here?"

"Yeah, I'll be right there," she said hanging up. I ordered two caramel mochas with half and half and whipped cream. Screw the extra calories, I wasn't about to settle for skim milk today.

"Kandice," I waved from the pickup counter.

"Why didn't you call me last night?" she asked.

"Everyone keeps asking me that. The answer is I don't know. I was scared and Robert showed up so I figured I was fine."

"Robert is one of the last people you should trust."

"Oh Kandice, he's fine, he just has a problem with his appendage, and since I don't intend on doing anything with it, I think it will be fine. I have to admit it was a nice surprise having him show up. At first, I was just annoyed, but the truth is it felt better knowing that if someone came in again, they would have to get through Robert first."

"Was there a note?" Kandice asked, sipping her coffee.

"Nope, not that I saw, just a tube of lipstick on my table."

"What are you going to do?"

"I don't know, I guess I'll go back and see if the guys are still home. Then I'll go to the police."

We took our coffees, got into Kandice's jeep, and drove back to my place.

Kandice and I walked up the steps to my door.

"Oh, by the way, I seemed to have lost my spare key. I need yours back until I can get another copy."

"You've lost your key too?"

"Yes, I'm sure I put it on the hook by the door where it always goes, but I went to lend it to

Alex last night and it wasn't there. So I need to use yours until I find it or make a new one."

"Okay, but you should think about changing your lock instead of making a new key. What if the killer is the one with your key?" Kandice asked, retrieving my key from her purse and handing it over. I took it, pocketing it for now.

"Great, I hadn't thought of that. I'm sure I just misplaced it." I hoped.

Alex was sitting on the couch watching TV when we came in. His arms crossed across his chest and a scowl on his face.

"Now that you've had your coffee and temper tantrum, can we discuss what happened last night?" He asked. Still staring at the TV.

I gave him a crusty look. "Yes, but is Robert still here?"

"No, he left."

"Oh." I was surprised.

"Did you happen to take a look at your patio yet?"

"No, why?" I asked, slowly.

"Well, go outside and have a look." He motioned towards the patio with his hand.

Leary about what I might see, I slowly went out to my patio. The words "Stay Out" were spray-painted in red across my patio.

"What the hell is this?" I shouted, "It's going to take forever to wash that off my deck."

Alex had a shocked look on his face.

"That's the first thing you think of when you see this?"

"Well yes, I love it out here and now it's ruined. Have I told you I hate strippers lately?" I could feel another "temper tantrum," as Alex put it, coming on.

Alex shook his head.

"Taryn, I'm calling David and having him come down here. This looks like a threat from the killer."

Before I knew it, Detective Parker and his crew were here combing through my house. Kandice had gone off to work and Alex was talking with David. So I called Robert and asked him to come by. To add to the chaos, I guess. I hadn't talked to him about what had happened the other night and I figured the police may want to talk to him too. I went out to sit on the steps and wait for Robert when I felt a rush of heat go through me. I looked up and saw Alex. He sat down beside me.

"You want to talk about last night?"

"There's not much to say. I woke up feeling like I was being watched, found the lipstick, and then Robert showed up."

"Tell me again why he was here?"

"I don't know, he said he was in the neighborhood and wanted to check-in. When I told him what happened, he refused to go home, so he stayed on the couch." I couldn't read Alex's expression, but I don't think it was a happy one.

"I'm sorry I was out so late. I shouldn't have left you," he apologized, softening a bit.

"It's fine. I have spent plenty of nights on my own. I don't know why I was so mad. Where did you go last night?" I asked, gently bumping my shoulder against his.

"I went to Joe's Bar to meet with a couple of people. I wish you would have called me, I would have been here in an instant."

"I know and should have," I agreed.

Robert came sauntering up the steps, looking fresh in khaki shorts and a red polo shirt.

"Alex," he greeted in a curt tone.

Alex acknowledged him with a slight nod of his head. He kissed me on the top of the head, got up, and went back inside. I wonder what happened between them once I left this morning? They had seemed friendlier while they drank all my coffee. Robert took Alex's place beside me and put his arm around me. I pushed it off.

"Not ready for that step in our friendship," I said.

"Oh sorry," he mumbled. "So…" He trailed off. Obviously not knowing what to say.

"So tell me about the other night. Start from when you got to the party," I finished for him.

"Why do you want to know? The message in the paint is clear, leave this to the police, Taryn." Robert replied, sternly.

"You're the only one I haven't talked to and I need to know what your story is," I insisted, ignoring his warning.

"Okay, I went to the party, had a few drinks, and paid for a few lap dances. She seemed really into me, so I talked to her afterward out on the balcony, and she agreed to come up to the room with me. She was so wild for me; she nearly wore me out. We were at it all night."

"Spare me the details of your animalistic instincts and just tell me the important stuff," I interrupted before he could continue.

"Are you jealous?" he smirked.

"No, just sickened at the thought of her naked."

"You really didn't like her."

"No, not really. Anyway, speaking of being sick, I heard you were sick that night and had to leave the party," I said, trying to get him back on track.

"No, I just needed a little fresh air," He argued, crossing his arms over his chest.

"When was the last time you saw her?"

"She was asleep in my bed, alive. She must have left the room while I was asleep."

"That's it? You have nothing more to tell?" I asked, frustrated that I couldn't get more out of him.

"Nope," He replied.

I groaned internally.

"What's with you and Alex then? When I left this morning you guys seemed fine, but now I feel like that's not the case."

"What do you mean?" He asked, innocently.

"Oh, Robert, I'm not a dummy, what's going on?" I asked, rolling my eyes.

"He asked me why I slept with the Vegas stripper and I said why not?" He said, flatly.

I punched him in the arm, "Oh, Robert, you're such an ass."

"What? I told you I couldn't help it," he squawked, rubbing his arm with a pout.

"You can leave now."

I pushed myself to my feet and went back into the house. Detective Parker seemed to be finishing up.

"Miss O'Kelly, here's my card, call me if anything else happens. In the meantime keep your doors locked and I'll have extra patrol on your street for a while."

Alex put his arm around me and I laid my head against his chest. "Now what?" I asked.

"You do your best to go back to normal. Plan your events and stay safe. I'll be here with you as much as possible."

Chapter 9

I could hear Marcy screeching in the background. "Dan, tell her I need to speak to her. Everything is fine and will move forward just as planned," I said.

"What!" she yelled into the phone.

"Marcy, I've called to let you know everything is moving forward just as we planned. There shouldn't be any more glitches."

"Glitches! Glitches! That stripper was a glitch?! I almost had to move the entire wedding because of her. I could kill Alex for even hiring her! That was not a glitch! It was a catastrophe!" Marcy ranted furiously.

I had to agree with her; it was a bride's worst nightmare.

"Marcy, please calm down. I promise your wedding will be everything you've ever wanted. The party rental is going to set up the tents and chairs tomorrow. I checked with both the caterer and the florist; they are ready to roll Saturday morning. Your band is coming out on

Thursday to do a practice run and sound check. It will all be fine."

I could hear her sniffling on the other end of the line.

"Marcy, I'm so sorry this happened, but don't cry."

"Taryn, do you know who killed her? I can't have a murderer running around my wedding. What if he offs one of my guests?" She worried.

"Marcy, I don't know, but the police are working on it. They'll catch him," I promised, trying to make her feel better.

"You have to find out who did it, Taryn; you have to stop the killer from coming to my wedding," she sniffed.

"Here's the thing, Marcy, the police are the investigators, not me. I wouldn't know where to begin," I replied softly.

"Taryn, I know you've already talked to all the groomsmen and Dan. Just keep digging. I know you'll figure it out."

"I'll see what I can do," I sighed.

"Please! Please! Please! Taryn, you have to!" She begged desperately.

"I'll see."

I disconnected with Marcy and had an even bigger task to complete; explaining all of this to my mother. I didn't want to call her, but if I took Alex with me, she wouldn't be able to lecture me. There was no way she would expose Alex to that, not as long as she thinks he could aid in the grandchildren department.

Poking my head out of my office, I could see Alex standing on the patio. It looked like he was on the phone, but I couldn't tell for sure. I walked up behind him and put my arms around his waist.

"Gotta go," he said, and he hung up with whoever he was talking to. He grabbed my hand and swung me around to face him. His dark honey eyes had a mischievous look about them, and the devilish grin he had on his face confirmed my thought. He leaned into me, brushing his lips against my ear. With a light flick of his tongue, he licked my earlobe and nuzzled my neck, sending a rush of heat throughout my body.

"You look hot. What does your schedule look like? I know a way we can kill time," he said as he nibbled on my earlobe and kissed me down my neck and across my shoulder. His hand had wandered under my shirt onto my breast. Things were really getting hot around my lower regions.

"I have a few things to get done today, but most importantly, I need to talk to my parents and would like you to come with me," I answered, trying to ignore my bodily desires.

That killed it. Alex removed his hand and fixed my shirt.

"When did you want to go?" he asked, clearing his throat.

"Now," I replied.

"I have a few things to do this afternoon, but maybe this evening we can pick up where we left off," he suggested as he leaned in and kissed me. I nearly fell over.

"I'd like that," I said softly, sinking into his arms.

We drove over to my parent's house, and my mother was cleaning. She cleans when she's mad, sad, frustrated, or anxious. Pretty much anytime she's overly stressed. I'm not talking about your average cleaning either. I'm talking toothbrushes and enough chemicals to start an investigation for chemical warfare. When Robert and I broke up, the house practically glowed in the dark it was so sparkling clean. My dad was ready to move to a hotel because even the air outside the house smelled like an indoor pool.

The house reeked of Pine-Sol, the weapon of choice today. My mother was on her hands and knees fine-scrubbing the woodwork.

"So you heard?" I asked my mother as we walked in.

"Yes, I heard! It was in the paper, and they mentioned your business too!" Mom looked up and saw Alex standing next to me.

"Oh, Alex, I didn't see you there."

"No problem, Mrs. O'Kelly. We came by to tell you what we know so far. We don't want you to worry about this," Alex smiled.

"Yeah, Mom, my business will be fine. The police have a few leads; they'll have this wrapped up in no time. The wedding planned for Saturday is still moving ahead as scheduled, and all of my other accounts have nothing to do with this or the Crystal Lake Estate," I said, reassuring my poor mom.

My mother looked stricken with relief. She let out a sigh.

"Taryn, you've worked so hard at making this dream of yours come true. I don't want this bad publicity to destroy this for you."

"I think it will turn out fine, Mom."

I wasn't about to let her know about last night's break-in.

"Stay for lunch. I'm making leftover pot roast sandwiches."

"Do you have leftover potatoes and gravy too?" I asked.

"Yes, but you'll ruin your sandwich if you put them in it."

I love making mashed potato, gravy, and pot roast sandwiches. I stuff all the leftovers inside the bread, and then I grill it up. It's delicious. My mom thinks it's gross and a waste of a good sandwich.

Alex leaned into me and whispered, "Lunch sounds good, but your sandwich sounds weird."

"Get used to it, baby. I am weird."

"I'm finding that out more and more."

"But you like it, right?" I asked teasingly.

"The jury's still out," he snorted.

"What?" I punched him in the shoulder and walked to the kitchen.

He caught up to me. "But it's looking favorable for you," he whispered in my ear.

I smiled, "Ha ha."

Mom made herself, Gramma, and Alex a sandwich. She told me I could make my own. She wasn't going to be the one to ruin a perfectly good sandwich. Gramps and Dad were out golfing and wouldn't be home for a while. They'd probably stop by the VFW for a beer before they got home too.

Alex tasted my sandwich. "Not bad," he said.

"I know. It's perfect."

We ate our lunch, and Gramma wanted to know everything about the murder. Gramma watches all the CSI shows, NCIS, Cold Case, and a lot of True TV. I was telling Gramma what happened while my mother periodically made sounds of disgust. She thinks those shows are gross, plus they give her nightmares if she does watch them. I'm kind of in the middle. I can watch most things like Gramma can, but not needles; they freak me out. I can't even watch when they draw my own blood, let alone something on TV. Some things give me nightmares, horror movies in particular. My mother says watching things like that desensitizes us. My gramma says she's too old to care.

We finished eating, and I cleaned up the kitchen for Mom. It's the least I could do since she fed us.

"Thanks for lunch."

I hugged my mom. I had a feeling the Pine-Sol would be put away, at least temporarily anyway.

Alex looked at me. "So what's up for the rest of the afternoon?" He asked as we headed out into the warm autumn air.

"I have some things to take care of at the office, mostly. What about you?" I asked.

"I've got some best-man duties," he replied, with a shrug.

"Will you drop me off at home then?"

"Sure, but it might cost you."

"I'll take that gamble," I laughed.

He leaned in and kissed me then opened the car door for me. He was always a gentleman, but I could see the bad-boy side of him coming out the longer we were together.

Back at the house, I thought about what Marcy had said. What if the police didn't find the killer before her wedding? It's not uncommon for investigations to last a long time. Maybe I would ask a few more questions. Business was light this week anyway. I certainly wasn't about to let some stupid threat scare me away, but where do I start? I already asked the groomsmen what they knew. Ella! I could talk to Ella. She may be able to give me Bambi's real name and where she lived.

I drove to the Hidden Closet. The afternoon had gotten warm, and I had picked a skirt, a three-quarter-sleeved shirt, and a sweater to wear. I wiggled out of my sweater, slung my purse over my shoulder, and walked into the shop. I spotted Ella; she was rearranging the lingerie section.

"Making room for your Halloween collection?" I asked as I walked up to her.

"Taryn, what brings you here? And yes, to answer your question, gotta get this place ready for the holidays."

"Well, I have a few questions about Bambi. I was hoping you could give me some information about her."

Ella mulled the question over. I was about ready to beg when she asked.

"What do you want to know?"

"What was her real name? Where did she live? Did she work anywhere else? Did she have any friends?" I fired off questions.

"Slow down. Let's go get my book. You know you're not the first person to come in here asking these questions. A couple of men and the PD have been here too."

"What did the men look like?"

"Well, one of them looked to be that tall, dark, handsome thing you had with you the other day."

"Alex?"

"Yeah, he was one of them. And the other one was damn good-looking too. Tall, blond, great tan, and a killer smile with those bright white teeth."

"Ugh... Robert!"

"You know both of them? How many good-looking guys are you hanging out with these days?" Ella asked, giving me a wink.

"Soon to be none if I don't start getting some answers. Were they together?"

"No, they came in separately."

"What did they ask you?"

"Well, the one you called Robert came in wanting to know how to contact her. He said they had had such a good time the other night that he'd like to see her again. I let him know that she had been murdered, and he looked genuinely upset. He wanted to know her real name and any information I could give him to remember her by."

"What? Robert was there when she was murdered. He could potentially be a suspect. Although I don't believe he's the killer. What information did you give him?"

"Nothing, I can't give information to every guy that comes in here wanting to know the whereabouts of the girls. The only thing I did do was give him her first name, Jessica, and tell him sorry for the loss," Ella shrugged.

"What about Alex? What did he want?" I asked.

"The same things you want."

"Did you tell him?"

"I had to. He had a warrant with him. It seems Jessica was hiding something."

"Warrant? Alex isn't a police officer," I said in confusion.

"It looked real to me, and I had already talked to another officer on the case," Ella replied, shrugging again.

Could Alex have faked a warrant? But why would he? Things just kept getting more confusing.

"Earth to Taryn, are you okay?" Ella asked, waving a hand in front of my face.

"Oh, yes, I am. I was just thinking," I said, stepping back.

"I should not be giving you this information, but since she is no longer with us, I guess it will be alright. Her name was Jessica Smith; here's her cell number. She lived at the Happy Trails Trailer Park #7. She was referred to me by another dancer. When she showed up to fill out an information sheet, she told me she was new in town and really needed some cash. I let her know how this all works and wished her luck. She had been picked several times and seemed thrilled every time I called with a new gig," Ella said, retrieving the information from her book.

"I'm sure she was," I muttered under my breath. "Okay! Thanks for the information, Ella." I started to leave. Ella touched my shoulder.

"Taryn, why did you want to know all this? You're not asking for trouble, are you?"

"Ella, I'm fine. I just need to piece this puzzle together myself. My client's wedding has been interrupted, and she's hysterical. She asked me to see what I could find out."

Ella pulled me close and hugged me.

"Be careful, honey; I don't like the way this all feels."

"I will, Ella. Thanks again."

I jumped in my truck and drove a short distance to the trailer park. I took Main over to 24th Street and onto Cedar, leading straight into the trailer park. Happy Trails Trailer Park was not happy at all. It was one of the sketchiest places to live in town. The police blotter always has something about this place. All the trailers are dilapidated. There are no street lamps, so it is probably a good idea to stay away after dark.

I wove my way through the park until I found #7. It was a rundown light-blue trailer with rickety-looking steps. A crappy old Ford Pinto was sitting out front. The olive-green paint was chipping away, leaving rust patterns all over the car. I sat in the truck for a minute, thinking about what to do next.

If I get out, my truck might be gone when I get back. That is, if I have the chance to come back. Or I could fall through the rickety steps and be gored by a piece of rotten, termite-infested wood. Maybe it's best to sit and wait for someone to come out. I looked around, and my decision was made for me. The roaches were already coming out. A man with a huge scar across his face stood outside of #8 staring at me. He had a cigarette hanging out of his mouth and was wearing an 80s muscle shirt revealing a chain of skulls tattooed down his left arm.

I heard a bang and jumped, shrieking loudly. Another winner of a guy was staring in through my passenger window. This one had a toothpick in his mouth. His head was shaved, and he had flame tattoos going up both arms. I rolled my window down slightly.

"Can I help you?" I asked in the strongest voice I could muster.

He didn't answer. He turned his head towards trailer #7 and yelled.

"Hey Billy, you got a visitor, you want me to entertain her or you gonna come out?"

A very large, fat man in a stained white shirt came out and stood on the rickety steps. I swear the porch bowed with his weight. I assumed this was Billy.

"What do ya want, bitch?" he yelled in my direction.

That's it! I went from scared to pissed in about two seconds. It's that Irish temper of mine. I wrenched open my door and stormed out of the truck.

"Who are you calling a bitch? Asshole!" I shouted at Fat Billy.

"You got a hot one, Billy," Scarface hollered.

"I want to know about Jessica. I was a friend of hers."

Flame Boy had moved to the front of the truck. I was a little nervous, so I placed my hand on my gun.

"What do you wanna know? That bitch owes me money. You here to pay it for her?" Billy grunted.

He didn't know she was dead? Had I beaten the police here?

"No! I need to know where she is."

"How the hell should I know? She probably ran off with that Shirley, or Cindy, whatever bitch. She took all her shit and left. I ain't seen her since last Friday. She owes me a month's rent."

He paused, looking me up and down. "You look like a fun time though. I bet you and me could have lots of fun working off her debt."

Scarface had moved closer and was slowly inching his way behind me. I reached for my door, but Scarface lunged and grabbed me.

He whispered, "Time for some fun," into my ear.

I could feel his hot breath on my neck. I tried to wiggle out of his arms, but he had a tight grip. I picked up my knee and back kicked him in the groin with my three-inch heels. He let go of me and toppled over in pain, moaning.

Flame Boy had made his way to the driver's side mirror. I wrenched open my door and scrambled into the truck. Flame Boy lunged at me, grabbing my door, attempting to keep me from closing it. I held tight to the door and started the engine. Flame Boy was still holding on to my door. I floored it out of there, dragging him until he let go. I felt a small bump under my back tire. I looked in the rearview mirror and Flame Boy was rolling on the ground, next to Scarface, holding his foot. I had run over him. Billy was standing over the two of them, waving his arms and screaming profanities.

I headed straight home. I needed to soak in a nice hot bath to get the roach cooties off of me and to say a few prayers of thanksgiving to my guardian angels. They had worked overtime today. I should probably see if there is a patron saint for idiots and thank him too. I was dumb, and the situation could have been a lot worse.

Chapter 10

I had shaken the fear of my Happy Trails incident off, said my prayers, and was relaxing in the tub when I heard the front door open.

"Hello," I hollered. Nothing, no answer. "Alex?"

The door swung open and Robert announced, "Hey baby, I'm home."

"GET OUT," I screamed, grabbing the shower curtain and trying to block myself.

"I just wanted you to know dinner is ready whenever you would like to come out."

He backed out, shutting the door as he left. What is wrong with him? I got out of the tub, grabbed my towel, and peeked out. Great, he hadn't closed my bedroom door. I dashed for the door and closed it. I put my pajamas on and reemerged from my room. Robert had brought Chinese for dinner. It was all set out on the table. He came out of the kitchen with an open bottle of wine and two glasses.

"Taryn, you're out. I know the last few days have been stressful, so I thought I'd bring you dinner and let you relax."

It would be more relaxing without him here, I thought. "Thanks." What else could I say to my weird ex?

"Robert, why are you doing all this? You come over unannounced, stay the night on my couch, bring me dinner, and flowers? What do you think is going to happen?"

"Nothing, I just want to be a good friend, that's all."

"Well, thanks for dinner. Hey, I have a question for you. Did you have any real connection with Bambi, or was it just the sex?"

"It was just sex. I felt nothing for her." Robert shrugged nonchalantly.

"How can you do that? It's supposed to be meaningful," I said, unable to understand his view on such an intimate act.

"I don't know; it's just my gift. Women want me, and I give them what they want."

"Oh, gag me, Robert. That's the lamest excuse for being a sex addict. You're more animal than man. Since she meant nothing to you, if she was alive you wouldn't want to see her again?"

"Nope."

Interesting, I thought, yet he had gone to Ella pretending to want to see her again. There was something he wasn't telling me, and I wasn't quite sure how to get it out of him.

"That seems a little cold, don't you think?"

"Nah," he shrugged his shoulders. "She was fun, but nothing special. Besides, she wasn't an innocent little angel, more like the naughty little demon."

"Why do you say that?"

Ew, gross, was what I was really thinking. If I could get him to keep talking, maybe I'd get another piece of what seems to be a never-ending puzzle.

"Oh, nothing really, I could just tell she had her share of skeletons in the closet. It doesn't surprise me that she got herself killed," he replied, opening the Chinese takeout boxes.

"What do you mean?" I asked, taking a sip of my wine. It was good.

"I'm just saying, she wasn't one to walk the straight and narrow."

"How do you know? Did you know her before the party?"

"Nope, why do you care anyway? I thought you hated all strippers," he said, arching one golden eyebrow.

"I do, but Marcy wants me to make sure that the killer doesn't attend her wedding," I explained, taking another sip.

"Sorry, can't help you. I have nothing to tell you. Do you like the wine? It reminds me of the Adesso you used to love."

"Um... yeah, I like it. Thank you."

I heard keys at the door. Alex walked in holding pizza and beer. He looked at Robert and me and went straight to the kitchen. The look on his face was not a pleasant one. More like an angry glare, most likely directed at Robert, I hoped. I got up and went after him. He put the pizza on the counter. I peeked at it. It was a spicy pizza from a little pizza shop on Main called Saucy Pies. They had the best pizza in town. Homemade dough and lots of homemade sauce. The Spicy Pizza had pepper jack and mozzarella cheese, topped with sliced spicy Italian sausage, pepperoni, jalapenos, and green chilies.

"What is he doing here?" he asked as he opened a beer. He took a long, hard swig and looked at me with his molten chocolate eyes. He was not happy.

"I don't know. He just showed up while I was taking a bath. He had dinner for me. He said he thought it might help because the last few days have been so stressful for me."

"He seems to be showing up a lot these days."

"Yeah, he says he wants me back in his life as friends."

"And do you want that?" he asked.

I wasn't sure how to answer that. "Um... I don't know. I don't want things to be awkward for us."

"Too late, baby, it is."

He leaned against the counter and took another swig of his beer.

My heart sank. I half-smiled at him. "I'm sorry."

I didn't know what else to say to him.

Alex leaned in and kissed me. "I can deal with it, but can you?"

"What do you mean?"

"You're going to have to set some boundaries. He can't just make himself at home whenever he wants. I can do it for you if that would be easier."

"No, I will do it, but not until we are done eating."

Robert waltzed into the kitchen as if nothing awkward was going on.

"I need more wine," he announced as he grabbed the bottle and went back to the table.

I shrugged my shoulders. I didn't know what to think.

"Do you want to bring the pizza out and join us?" I asked. "I'll share my House Lo-Mein with you."

I grabbed the pizza, and Alex followed with his beer and a plate.

I thought I heard Alex mutter, "This should be fun," under his breath.

"You had the same idea I see," said Robert. "I like how you cook."

"I can cook quite well actually when I have the time," Alex growled.

"So can I," boasted Robert, "but I know how Taryn loves her Lo-Mein, I know what wine she drinks, and what chocolates she loves. Do you?"

I sank further into my chair . This was not relaxing. This was a nightmare. I had to stop the power struggle, now.

"Okay," I said, "how about we talk about something else?"

"What would you like to talk about?" asked Robert.

"I don't know? The weather?" I suggested.

"It was nice today." He picked-up his chopsticks with a stupid grin.

Alex just stared at us, not saying anything, but clearly annoyed.

Dinner finally ended, and Robert left. Alex and I snuggled on the couch and started to watch Indiana Jones: The Last Crusade when he got a phone call. He took the call outside.

"I have to go," he said, as he came back in, "but I'll be back in a little bit."

"Okay, where are you going?" I asked.

"Joe's Bar. I have to meet with a client. See you in a little bit. I won't be as late as last time, I promise."

He kissed me on the top of my head, and then he was gone. I sat there for a minute, thinking. Alex had been receiving a lot of phone calls lately, and he had been by to see Ella too. I grabbed my phone on my way to my room. I was going to get dressed and spy on him. I called Kandice and told her what I wanted to do. She was game and said she'd pick me up in five.

Kandice was out front, right on time. I grabbed my coat and keys and locked my door. Which reminded me I still hadn't found my spare key. I put that on my mental list of things to do tomorrow. Find that key.

As we drove down Main Street to Joe's Bar, I was having second thoughts. I turned to

Kandice. "Maybe this was a stupid idea. I should be able to trust Alex."

"Now we'll know for sure," Kandice said.

As I got out of the Jeep, I could feel my stomach churning. What was I going to say if Alex saw me? Realizing that this was truly a half-baked plan, I turned around to get back into the jeep when Kandice grabbed my arm.

"Oh no, we're going in. He's been out too many times to let this go unchecked."

"This is his job," I whined. Even as I said it, I didn't know if I believed it.

"He flies for God's sake. Why does he have to meet his potential passengers secretly and late at night?" She hissed back.

"I don't know, but maybe we should respect his privacy."

"Hell no! We're down here and we're going in."

Kandice linked arms with me and escorted me into the bar. It was very crowded. Which was a good thing, since I didn't want to get caught. We maneuvered our way through pockets of people to the back of the bar. There were a couple of booths in the back. We could hide in one and see most of the bar. Once settled in, we ordered a couple of beers and sat tight.

"I don't see him. He left before I called you. He should be here," I said quietly, carefully glancing around.

"Do you see why this was a good idea now? He obviously made a stop on the way," Kandice replied, taking a swig of her beer.

We sat for a while, but before Alex could show up, Flame Boy and his brood of wannabe gangsters came into the bar. His foot was bandaged up with what looked to be a temporary cast.

"Oh, crap! Kandice, we've gotta go!" I whispered in alarm.

"No! He hasn't shown up yet."

"Nope, but someone else has, and he can't see me."

"What? Who?"

"A guy I sort of hit and ran today," I squished up my face and winced.

"You ran over someone and I'm just now finding out about it!" She gasped, looking weirdly excited and offended.

"Yeah. I'll tell you the whole story once in the car, but we need to go now!" I grabbed my purse, and we started to weave our way back to the door when someone grabbed my hair and jerked me backward. I turned around; Flame Boy was standing there with his posse of misfits. He pulled me in close. His breath reeked of cigarettes and booze.

"Hey bitch, Billy wants his money, and he wants it from you now. He don't like to be messed with."

"Tell Billy that he'll never get his money. Jessica is dead, and I don't owe him anything." My voice cracked a couple of times, but I tried to sound strong.

He tightened his grip on my arm and stared at me with his cold dark eyes. I tried to pull away, but he wasn't about to let me go. He started to growl something at me when Kandice punched him in the face, sending him backwards into his buddies.

I'm not sure what happened next exactly, but a fight broke out in the bar. Fists were flying, and grown men were rolling on the floor. The spectators had managed to line the walls, staying out of the line of fire, and somehow we narrowly escaped. The police would be there any minute.

Back in the jeep, I told Kandice the whole Happy Trails unhappy experience. She laughed so hard she started choking.

"I don't think it was that funny," I grumbled

"I do! Now that idiot will have a broken nose to match his broken foot," she said, continuing to choke.

I sat quietly for the rest of the ride home. Maybe I shouldn't get involved any further. Now I had an idiot gangster wannabe and a murderer mad at me. I'm guessing that's not such a good thing. But then again, why should I let a little spray paint and trailer trash scare me? We pulled up to my house, and I started to get out.

"Taryn, you okay?" Kandice asked.

"Oh yeah. Nothing in my life is making sense right now, that's all."

"Personally, I think Alex makes sense even if he is hiding something. Robert needs to jump off a cliff, and this murder thing will be behind you by the end of the week. Stop worrying so much," Kandice said cheerfully. It was nice how she tried to reassure me, but it didn't work.

"We don't know if Alex is hiding anything, and Robert does not need to jump off a cliff," I said.

"Yes, he does."

"No, he just needs to find someone else to follow around."

"You mean stalk," Kandice said in a snarky voice.

"No, he's not stalking me. He's just trying to be my friend. That's all."

"You think what you want, and I'll do the same. As for Alex, let it be. Just have fun with him and see where it goes. Everybody has a secret or two. At least you know he's not the murderer; you can't say that for sure about Robert."

"Yeah, I guess."

I got out of the Jeep and waved Kandice off. I opened the door to find Alex sitting on the couch watching TV.

"You're back already? I thought I wouldn't see you for a while," I asked, feeling surprised.

"I told you I wouldn't be out late again," he smiled.

"Did your meeting go well?"

"Yep. Where did you and Kandice go?"

How'd he know I was with Kandice? I hadn't told him. Was he following me? Lost in thought, Alex called me back.

"Taryn, are you okay? You look upset. I saw you sitting in the jeep talking for a while out there."

"Yeah. I'm fine," I said.

No, I'm not, I thought to myself. I'm paranoid. Kandice is right; I need to have fun with Alex and stop thinking about this murder.

"Hey, I'm going to change. I'll be right back."

I went to my room to freshen up. I wanted the bar smell off of me. I didn't want to think about the murderer, Robert, or the gangsters. I just wanted a moment with Alex. He had said he would like to see the teddy again. So, I thought, why not? I showered, slipped on the sexy lingerie, and came out of my room feeling a little silly. Alex didn't seem to mind.

"Wow. You look hot. You realize I won't be able to control myself now."

"That's what I intended," I said, trying to sound sexy and not stupid.

He grabbed me and pulled me to him. His tongue was soft, his lips delicious, and his hands moved all over me. He kissed me long, moved down my neck, across my collarbone, and down to my breast. His warm hands squeezed my breasts; he sucked my nipple into his mouth, and his tongue danced around it. He scooped me into his arms and took me to the bedroom. As he carried me, every nerve in my body tingled with anticipation. Stripping me of the little clothing I had on, he laid me down on the bed. He quickly removed his clothing. Every inch of him was hard, his eyes filled with desire and tenderness. His touch was like fire against my skin as he trailed kisses along the curve of my waist. I ran my fingers through his thick hair, pulling him closer. His hands were skilled and tender, exploring every inch of my body, leaving trails of intense yearning behind. As he claimed my lips once more, we surrendered to each other. He thrust himself into me, binding us together in a dance of passion. The rhythm of our bodies became a melody of its own, lost in the depths of each other's embrace.

Chapter 11

I woke up feeling quite satisfied after enjoying the best night of my life. Alex was amazing, and I was ready to run away with him. He was already making breakfast, so I decided to shower. I got dressed in jeans and a V-neck t-shirt. I was going to Crystal Lake this morning to help with the setup of tents and chairs.

When I came out of the room, Alex had just finished setting the table. I came up behind him and wrapped my arms around him. He grabbed my hand and pulled me around in front of him and kissed me. His kisses could turn you to Jell-O instantly. Mmm… is all I could say.

"Good morning, beautiful."

"Morning. Breakfast smells good."

"You smell good. We could skip breakfast and go back to bed, you know," he suggested, wiggling his eyebrows and smirking.

"Tempting, very tempting, but I have a lot of work to do today. Plus, you worked hard to make this delicious breakfast."

"Pancakes, eggs, bacon, and hash browns," he said, grinning.

"Yum, thank you." I was starving.

"What are your plans for today?" He asked.

"I have to help with the party rental setup. Do you want to come along?"

"I could do that."

"Good. You can help make sure it looks good. I don't want anything else to go wrong for Marcy. Has anyone stayed out there since the murder?"

"Jason and Ryan have. Dan and Marcy went to the hot springs like you suggested and have stayed at a B&B the last two nights."

"Marcy is going to swing by to check on things after lunch today. I hope it all looks exactly like what she pictured."

"Me too. That woman always finds something to complain about," Alex said.

"Well, after what happened, let's hope she has nothing left to complain about. That was awful."

"True, I'm going to shower, then we can leave."

"Okay, I will clean up breakfast."

He leaned in and kissed me. We kissed for a few minutes until I pulled away. We had to stop, or else the plans for the day would have changed drastically.

We arrived at Crystal Lakes about 15 minutes before the party rental was due. As always, Sam opened the door and escorted us in. Something was different about him, but what was it? He had on the same hot suit and tie he always wore.

"Alex, Taryn, come in," he said, but not in the same manner he usually used. Hmm. Maybe he was just having a bad day, hard to be formal and upbeat all the time.

"You go on ahead. I will be there in a minute," Alex said.

I went to the kitchen. I don't know why exactly, but I hadn't been in there since that horrible night. I know the police searched everything. What if they missed something?

I looked around hoping to find some clue. Of course, they didn't miss anything. They're professionals. Did they check Robert's room? Alex hadn't come to find me, which was probably a good thing since I was nosing around doing exactly what I sort of promised him I wouldn't do. I ran up the stairs to Robert's room, opened the door, and snuck in. I closed the door behind me, hoping no one would notice me. The bed was made, and the room looked like it had been cleaned. Mrs. Williams must have come in. Darn, there was nothing to find here.

Back downstairs, I heard Sam open the door; the party rental company was here. Oh, crap. I'll have to continue looking around later. I went to greet them and then led them out to the grassy area. "The tents need to be close to the lake on either side of the platform. We would like rows of fifteen by six under each tent. The platform needs to be right in front of the lake with the mountain peaks centered in the background." Once things were rolling, I decided to sneak away to see if I could find out anything else about that awful night.

I headed for the balcony, where I had seen Robert. The view was breathtaking. Stay focused, I told myself. I looked around the deck, under and around the plants, and along the railing. I was just about to leave when something shined in the sunlight. It was a blue sequin. I didn't feel like it helped much. Since I knew Bambi's costume had them on it, I put it in my pocket anyway.

I went back to check on the rental company, and they were doing just fine. I still didn't know where Alex had gone to. That was okay because I had two more places I wanted to check. I quietly snuck into the cinema room to see if anything from the party was still there. Of course, Mrs. Williams had gotten to that too. The room was spotless. I was beginning to feel like this was a lost cause, knowing my last destination most likely would turn up nothing.

I knocked on the office door. No Answer. I let myself in and cracked the door, hoping to be able to hear if someone was coming. I wasn't sure what I was looking for, but I hoped I'd know once I found it. There was nothing that looked to be of interest on the floor or the shelves. I went behind the desk. There were a couple of filing cabinets, but I didn't think I needed to look in those. A voice cleared, and I jumped.

"Miss O'Kelly, can I help you?"

"Oh, Sam, um, Sir, you startled me."

"What are you doing in here?"

"I...." Think, Taryn, think. "I was um, looking for you. I left my notes about the wedding at home and hoped maybe I could find the copy I gave you?"

Sam came around the desk. He opened one of the cabinets and pulled out the file for Marcy's wedding.

"Is this what you would like?" He held out the folder.

"Um, yes. I just needed to double-check what direction the boat was coming from."

I opened the folder and skimmed through it. Hoping he bought my story, I closed the folder.

"Thanks, now I can continue the setup." I turned to leave but was pulled back by an icy cold hand.

"Miss O'Kelly ... " Sam was interrupted.

"Taryn, there you are. I've been looking for you," Alex said as he came in. Sam let my arm go. A sigh of relief rushed through me. I walked over to Alex, thinking to myself Thank you, God. I don't think Sam was too happy with my being in his office. I grabbed Alex's arm and pulled him out, calling back to Sam, "Thanks, that helped a bunch."

"What did you need help with?" Alex asked, allowing me to pull him along.

"Oh, just a couple of details for the wedding. Where have you been?"

"I packed a few more clothes for your place and talked to Sam for a little while."

We walked out to the back deck. The rental company was doing a fabulous job. This really was going to be perfect. My cell phone rang. "Amazing Memories! This is Taryn," I answered.

"Taryn, it's Marcy."

"Marcy, hi, everything is going great. I think you're going to be very pleased."

"That's good, Taryn. I'm not going to come out today. I'm much too busy; just make sure it's right. Okay, gotta go."

"Okay? Bye? That was weird. Marcy is not coming out," I told Alex.

"Dan, the guys, and I are hanging out later this afternoon. Maybe she and the girls are shopping or something."

"Yeah, maybe. Oh well."

Once we got the setup done and everything looked good, Alex and I took off. I had phone calls to make, and Alex had guy time to get to. Back at the house, I checked on the flowers, caterer, and band; they all were set. I looked at the time. It was after 1:00, and I hadn't had lunch. My stomach rumbled. Giselle must have felt a rumble too because when I opened the fridge she was at my feet meowing. I pulled out some turkey lunch meat, gave Giselle a chunk, and made a sandwich. I went to sit on the patio but remembered the paint and decided to stay inside instead. I needed to get that cleaned up.

I wanted to see Ella today. She might know who this Cindy person is. Maybe I could find out who Bambi was connected to at the party that night. I finished my lunch and said goodbye to my cat, who was now giving herself a bath in the middle of my living room rug. Looking put out by the interruption, she made her best effort to allow me to give her a goodbye pat. I locked the door and went down the steps to the truck. I needed to call Scotty about my key too, I thought. I better do that now. I dialed his number and got his voicemail, so I left a message.

"Hey Scotty, it's Taryn. I seem to have lost my spare key and was hoping I just never got it back from you. Please check and let me know. Thanks, love you."

With that taken care of, I drove to the Hidden Closet again.

Ella was sitting behind the checkout counter. "Hi Ella," I waved as I came through the door.

"Taryn," she said in a cheery voice. "How was Happy Trails?"

"Not very happy. Jessica lived with a horrible guy. Apparently, she owed him rent and hasn't been seen for a couple of weeks. Do you know a woman named Cindy? She was supposed to be staying with her."

"I think I know who you're talking about."

"Can you give me her number?"

"I don't know, Taryn. You know the policy. With Jessica, it didn't matter too much since she is no longer with us, but Cindy still works through me," Ella said hesitantly.

"I know, but I was hoping we could bend that rule. I won't tell anyone who gave me her number. Promise. If she asks, I'll tell her Jessica gave it to me."

"Taryn, I do want to help you. I like you; you're a good girl, but I don't like the way this all feels. It's against my policy too."

"What if it helps catch the murderer? What if the murderer has something against strippers and comes after another one of the girls?"

Even as I said it, I didn't really believe it, at least I hoped that wasn't what the murderer was up to.

"You don't think that this guy is a serial killer, do you?" She asked, her eyes wide.

"I don't know; I hope not, but I would like to find out what's going on. Besides, if I find out anything worthwhile, I'll go straight to the police."

"All right, here's her number, but you can't tell her you got it from me," Ella relented. She wrote the number down for me.

"Deal! Thanks, Ella. You're great. Oh, one more thing; has either of the guys that came in the other day come back?"

"No."

"Good. Thanks again." I hugged her and left.

Back in the truck, I was so excited. This is the next step. I called Cindy. Lucky for me, she answered, and she was willing to see me. I'm sure my story of being great friends with Jessica and wanting to retrieve any personal items for her family helped a little. Dear God, please forgive me, I prayed on the way there. I had been lying a lot lately, and that's not something I usually do.

Cindy lived in a townhouse towards the edge of town; the Pinewood Townhomes. They were beautiful homes neatly tucked into the forest surrounded by pine trees. They had that country rustic look, like little log cabins. I went and knocked on #4, and a very beautiful blond opened the door. She was tall, thin, and had sparkling clear blue eyes.

"I'm looking for Cindy," I said.

"I'm Cindy. You must be Taryn."

"I am."

"Come in, so you were friends with Jessica?"

"Yes, she and I go way back."

"I'm surprised you could tolerate her that long."

"Well, you know, sometimes the time itself is what creates tolerance."

"I suppose," she said as she eyed me questioningly.

I was getting a little nervous. I've never been a very good liar; that's one of the reasons I don't do it often. That and, of course, the fact that God disapproves.

"Would you like some water, coffee, anything?" She asked.

"Water would be nice, thank you," I agreed. She disappeared into the kitchen. I looked around her living room. It was exquisitely decorated. Everything was perfectly placed, not a bit of dust or clutter. It looked like an expensive show home.

"When was the last time you saw her?" I asked as Cindy handed me my water.

"The night she got herself killed. She was getting ready for her show. I had just found out she slept with Frank, my boyfriend, and I was furious. I wanted to kill her right there," Cindy growled.

"Oh, Cindy, I'm sorry. She tried to sleep with mine too. How did you find out?" I asked, I could sympathize with that, plus it wasn't even a lie.

"Frank had come home feeling frisky, and during our romp, the idiot asked me if I was going to charge him for additional sexual favors. I knew he had slept with her. She had come home a few nights earlier telling me about some guy she had conned into paying her for 'additional sexual favors'. She was so proud of her new scam. She'd lure a guy in, a very drunk one, after her show, and during their fun, she'd start charging for the dirty stuff."

I can't believe guys fell for it, I thought to myself. "That's awful."

"I asked Frank right then and there if he had slept with her, and he confessed everything. So, like any self-respecting woman, I screamed, yelled, and threw things at him before I kicked him out. When Jessica got home, I confronted her about it with the same level-headed behavior. She laughed, grabbed her bag, and left. That was the last time I saw her. I don't know what hurt more, losing Frank to her or letting her stay here for free until she found her own place."

"Cindy, I don't know what to say. She was a tornado of destruction everywhere she went."

"Come with me; I'll show you her room. I need to clean it out. I just haven't felt like doing it."

Jessica's room was a pigsty. There were clothes, shoes, and takeout boxes everywhere. "Ew! Have the police contacted you?" I asked.

"No, why?" She arched an eyebrow.

"I was just wondering. They talked to me, and last I knew, they still didn't have much on the case. They might want to see this room. It could have clues to who wanted her dead."

"Didn't everyone who ever met her want her dead?"

"You're probably right, except I'm sure there are only a few people who would actually do it."

"Do you want to call them?" Cindy asked.

"Let's look through it first, then we'll call," I said.

We carefully sifted through the filth. Jessica really didn't have that much stuff; it was just that all she had was thrown everywhere and the amount of trash was unreal. In the closet hung her dancing outfits. Cindy walked over and scooped them up.

"I'll keep these as payment. I can have them dry-cleaned to get rid of her cooties and have them altered."

She placed them in a bag and hauled them off to her room. They probably didn't have any evidence in them anyway, I thought.

While Cindy was gone, I happened to look under her bed and found a wad of money taped to the mattress. I didn't want Cindy to find that, or she'd keep it too, and that could be evidence. When she came back to the room, I was looking at the nightstand. Jessica had a small notepad by the phone. On it, there were two numbers. One said pick-up beside it. I pulled out my cell and took a picture of it. It could be important.

"Well, I don't see anything else, let's call the police," I said. "When they're done, I'll help you clean up this mess.

I pulled out Detective David Parker's card and called his number.

"Detective Parker? Hi, it's Taryn. I'm at Jessica's last known address. I think you might want to come here and check out her room."

"What are you doing at her place, Miss O'Kelly?"

"Uh? I... Just helping?"

I stepped out of the room, hoping Cindy wouldn't hear me.

"Look, David, there's a wad of cash taped under her bed and a couple of numbers on the notepad near her bed. I thought you might be interested. I'm at the Pinewood Townhomes, number 4. Are you coming down or should I let her roommate clear out the room?"

"NO! Don't touch anything. I'll be right there."

"Thank you," I said in a cheery voice. He may not have been happy with me, but at least he was coming to see what I found.

I went back to the room and found Cindy sitting on the bed crying.

"Cindy, are you okay?"

"No, I miss Frank, and I hate that stupid cow, Jessica," she sobbed.

Tears were pouring down her cheeks.

I didn't know what to say. Wait! Robert! She didn't have to know it wasn't Jessica he cheated with. I sat down next to Cindy and shared my Robert story. Letting her think it was the stripper, Bambi, all along. I explained to her that she was worth more than what Frank had treated her as. Moving on, although painful, was a refreshing journey. Now I'm with a wonderful man whom Jessica tried to get her claws into. He had turned her down for me. You'll find someone who knows what you are worth, someone who cannot be tempted. She seemed somewhat cheered up.

Detective David Parker was knocking at the door. Officer Ballenger was with him. I introduced them to Cindy, and we all headed upstairs to Jessica's room. Officer Ballenger pulled Cindy aside to ask her some of the same questions I asked her and to get her statement. I had forgotten to ask her what she was doing that night. Darn. I strained to hear what she was telling him. I couldn't hear anything worthwhile, so I went over to David. He gave me a crusty look.

"Why are you so upset with me?" I asked.

"Why do you think?" He huffed.

Before I could answer, he bent down and looked under the bed. Finding the cash I already knew was there, he pulled it out. I looked over at Cindy. She looked shocked and ready to explode all at once. I felt bad for her. Jessica really left a tidal wave for her to clean up. David continued to search the room, and he didn't appear to find anything else except the numbers I found too.

"Miss O'Kelly, can I speak to you for a minute? I need to ask you some questions."

He pulled me aside so that no one could hear us.

"How did you know where she was living?" He demanded.

"I talked to a friend," I replied vaguely

"What friend?" He sounded impatient.

"I'm not at liberty to reveal her name."

"Do you think this is some kind of game, Miss O'Kelly?" he growled.

"No."

"Then answer the question!"

"I can't, but I called you when I found the place, didn't I? That should be good enough."

I could see the anger in his eyes, and suddenly he relaxed as if defeated.

"Taryn, I need you to stay out of this. I promised Alex I'd do my best to keep you safe. Your snooping around puts you in danger. The threat you got was not some kind of joke." He sounded more concerned at this point.

"Why doesn't he just keep me safe? Speaking of Alex. Why did he have a warrant for the Hidden Closet? Why was he out so late the night the intruder came? You're his friend; tell me what's going on," I demanded. They were all hiding things from me, and I didn't appreciate it.

"I can't answer those questions."

"Can't or won't?" I glared at him.

"Both."

He gently placed his hand on my shoulder. "Just trust him; that's all I can tell you," he said.

"It seems neither of us can answer the questions we each have," I said, shoving his hand off my shoulder.

"Looks that way."

"But why can't we work together?" I whined.

"Because you are not a cop!" he snapped.

"I may not be a cop, but I found this place before you guys did."

I could see another flash of anger behind his eyes, and just as quickly as it came, it was gone.

"Miss O'Kelly, thank you for your help in this matter; however, in the future, please leave the investigations to the professionals. Good afternoon."

He turned and stalked away.

Once they had left, I helped Cindy clean out Jessica's room. By the time we had all the trash out, there were only a couple of boxes of clothes left. She had nothing that appeared to be sentimental or valuable to her family. I took the boxes anyway since that had been my ruse to get here in the first place. I'd call Detective Parker and ask him what to do with it. I'm sure he'll love that.

"Thank you, Taryn," Cindy said as she helped load the boxes into my truck. "How someone as nice as you could ever be friends with that horrible woman I'll never understand." She shook her head and hugged me goodbye.

I said goodbye and got into the truck to drive home. My brain had gone on autopilot, so by the time I arrived at my driveway I was surprised to be home already. It's scary how that can happen. You can drive to your destination and not even remember the trip. I sat in the truck for a few minutes longer, still thinking. I thought I heard Officer Ballenger say he had counted $10,000 taped up under that bed. I must have heard wrong. Nobody has that kind of money lying around. She owed rent to Billy; if she had that, she could have paid him and gotten his minions to leave her alone. Why didn't she pay him?

I was exhausted from cleaning up the stripper's mess. "I hate strippers," I grumbled to no one in particular as I hauled myself out of the truck. I put the boxes in my garage and went up the steps into my house, locking the door behind me. I needed a shower; Jessica's room was disgusting, and I wanted all her cooties off of me.

Chapter 12

Feeling clean again, I went to the kitchen to start dinner but was interrupted by a knock at the door. It was Robert. I had almost forgotten what a day without Robert felt like. Normal.

"Hi Robert," I said in a monotone voice as I opened the door.

"What, not happy to see me?" He grinned widely and leaned on the door frame.

"No, not really," I hissed.

He pushed his way in. "So, busy day?" he asked.

"I guess so."

I reluctantly closed the door. Robert was like a cockroach. Damn near impossible to get rid of, and always came back. It wasn't worth the energy to throw him out just so he could come right back.

"What did you find out about Jessica?" he asked, trotting over to bully Giselle with cuddles.

"Why would I find anything out about her?" I asked, I felt a bit suspicious about his asking.

"I know you better than that, Taryn. You haven't given up." He gave me a smirk before cooing at and lifting my cat into his arms.

"How can I give up something I never started?" I asked.

"Please, don't try to lie to me Taryn. I see right through you. You were never a very good liar."

Giselle was giving me a pleading look as Robert hugged and kissed her.

"I should be better now. I did learn from the best," I said, placing my hands on my hips.

"Keep trying, baby," he said, tapping me on the nose.

"Fine, I've found out nothing. Why do you care?" I said, reaching for my cat.

"Just curious."

"Well, I am too. So here's a question for you. Have you ever paid for sex?"

"No! Why would you ask me that?" He replied, sounding offended.

"Just curious, like you," I said. "What about being tricked into additional sexual favors for a fee?"

"Taryn, I don't know what you're talking about."

"Really?" I could see he was getting angry. I definitely struck a nerve.

"No! Prostitution is illegal. I wouldn't risk all I have for a prostitute."

"You'll just risk all you have for the illegal act of adultery."

"That's not illegal."

"It is according to God."

"Not if my gift is great sex."

"I wouldn't call it great."

Even as I said it, I knew it was a lie, but Alex was fantastic, and I was getting really angry.

"And what do you have to compare it to?" He sneered.

I didn't need to answer his question; the look on his face said he knew.

"You want great? I'll give you awesome!"

He grabbed me, pressed his body against mine, and kissed me hard. I tried to slap him, but his grip was too strong for me to break free. He threw me onto the couch, pinning me against it with his body. I tried to push him off of me, but he was too powerful. As I was struggling to get free, Alex came into the room and saw what I could only imagine as a horrifying sight of Robert and me on the couch. He pulled Robert off of me, punched him in the face, turned to me, and handed me my key.

"This was not what I meant when I said you needed to set some boundaries," he said, as he stormed out of the house.

"Alex! Wait, it's not what you think," I ran out after him.

Alex whirled around, glaring down at me. "What is it then? You play this hurt, untrusting girlfriend, yet your ex is always around. What's really going on?" he snarled.

"He just keeps coming by, and I sort of said you were a better lover than him."

A spark in his eye and a slight smile formed on his face, and then it was gone.

"Then why was he on you when I walked in?"

"He was going to make me see how great he was. I'm actually glad you walked in. I have never seen him behave this way. I'm not sure what he would have done."

"If that's true, I'm glad you're okay."

"It is true." Tears started to well in my eyes.

"You should stay away from Robert. I don't trust him." He turned and started to walk away.

I grabbed his arm. "Here, take this back." I held out my key.

"Please."

We stood in silence for a moment. He hesitantly took the key, glancing down at it for a moment. He looked like he wanted to say something, but instead he nodded and turned to leave.

I went back into the house. Robert was sitting on the couch watching TV.

"GET OUT!" I screamed. I picked up a pillow from the couch and threw it at him. "Get out!"

"Taryn, come on," he said, raising his hands pleadingly.

"No, get out! You have caused enough problems."

"Well, if you ask me, he's too sensitive. What you need is a real man. One who gets what he wants. Always." He sauntered out my door.

I collapsed onto the couch and started to cry. I could call Kandice, but I didn't really want to talk to anyone. After what seemed like hours, my tears dried up and I couldn't cry anymore. I went to the kitchen, heated up some leftovers, ate, and went to bed. I needed to sleep this off and figure it out tomorrow. Scarlet O'Hara was on to something. Tomorrow the problems would still be there to be dealt with, so why worry about them now?

I woke up early, and the house was freezing. Grabbing my robe, I headed for the pellet stove. As I came down the hall, I could feel the blood drain from my face. I grabbed the wall to catch myself. In the middle of my table was a meat thermometer missing its cord. Next to it was a note. I looked over at my patio, and the door was standing wide open. I rushed over and closed it. I could still feel a draft; my front door was standing open too. I grabbed the phone and called the police while I closed and locked my front door. I was scared to open the note, so I waited until Detective Parker showed up. I called Alex, but he didn't answer, of course. I started the coffee, and before I could even pour a cup, Detective Parker was at my door.

"Miss O'Kelly, tell me what happened," he said.

"I woke up freezing, so I came out to start the pellet stove when I noticed the horrifying gift on my table. I noticed the reason I was freezing. It was because both my patio and front doors were wide open," I explained as I opened the door and let him inside.

"Have you read the note?"

"No, I waited for you."

David walked over to the table, gloved his hand, and picked up the note. "I warned you once, now twice; the next time you'll be on ice."

I started to feel faint, and I stumbled. David caught me as I was crashing to the floor. The next thing I knew, I was lying on the couch.

"Miss O'Kelly, are you alright?" David asked.

"Yeah, I don't know what happened," I groaned, slowly sitting up. My ears were ringing, and my head throbbed.

"You fainted. I caught you before you hit the floor," he replied.

"Thanks. Sorry."

"It's fine. This threat is pretty serious. I'm going to have someone watch your house for the next couple of days."

"Thank you. Um, David. Have you talked to Alex?"

"Yeah, he stayed at my place last night," David sighed.

"How is he?" I asked hesitantly, shifting my weight from side to side.

"He's good. He's working on some stuff right now. He cares about you. He won't be happy to hear this."

David wrinkled his face in thought.

"Can you tell him I'm sorry? I don't know what he told you, but nothing did or ever will happen with Robert. Please tell him," I wrung my hands awkwardly.

"I'll see what I can do," he said as he closed his notepad.

"Thanks. Do you think those numbers I found have anything to do with the case?" I ran my hand across the edge of the couch.

"Miss O'Kelly, I'm not at liberty to discuss the case with you, and I think you should stop worrying about it. The note is clear; you have obviously upset the killer. Your personal investigation will only make things harder for us."

"I helped you yesterday. Without me, you would not have found that money or the numbers," I said, placing my hands on my hips.

"Miss O'Kelly, my team would have done it without you; I have no doubt about that!" he snapped.

"Did you tell Alex about yesterday?" I asked.

"I didn't need to; he already knew."

"How?" I was confused.

"Miss O'Kelly, if there is nothing else to tell me about the current event, I must go," David said as he edged towards the door.

"Detective, I do have one more thing. I sort of told Cindy I was a lifelong friend of Jessica's. So now I have all her stuff in my garage."

I sat silently, waiting for a minute. He did not respond, but his face said it all. He was clearly amused and bewildered with me all at once.

"It was the only thing I could think of to get into her house."

"Great. Let's get the stuff," he said in an agitated voice.

The police packed up their stuff, took Jessica's belongings, and left. I was about to call Kandice when she showed up. She was bearing gifts of bagels and coffee. Something was up.

"Hey, Kandice? What's going on?" I asked, letting her in.

"Is Alex here?" She asked, looking sympathetic.

"No, I have to tell you about that," I sighed.

"Good," she said, talking right over me. "I saw him last night with another woman."

"What?"

"I know. I'm so sorry. I hate that I told you to go for it with that jerk." She kept rambling.

"I slept with him," I said flatly.

"When? You didn't call me? I pushed you into the arms of that pig; the least you could have done is call with the details!" she screeched, grabbing me and pulling me into her, squeezing me.

"I wanted to, but a lot happened yesterday, and I'm still trying to process it all," I said, breaking her embrace and rubbing my temples.

"Was it good?" Kandice asked. Despite the situation, she still wanted all the dirty details.

"Kandice, I thought he was a pig?" I groaned.

"Pig or not. I want to know if he was worth it," she grinned.

"Good grief. Yes, he was fantastic. It was like nothing I have ever experienced. But back to the point, you saw him with someone else?"

I needed to keep her on task. I needed to know if Alex really was trash.

"Yes. Trey and I were at Joe's Bar and Grill. He had just gotten back into town from one of his trips. While we were sitting there catching up, Alex walked in. I watched him walk over to one of the booths, to a woman with long blond hair and a smoking body, but not as hot as yours of course."

I rolled my eyes. "Please. Don't sugarcoat it."

"What? It's true," she praised. "Alex whispered something in the blond's ear, and she smiled. She took his arm, and they left. I jumped out of my seat and went after them. I followed them several blocks down Main until they went into Pepe's Italian Market. I saw them get seated for dinner, then realized I had left Trey sitting in the bar with no clue as to where I had gone. Knowing I wouldn't be able to spy much with them in there, I went back to Trey. He was a little confused, but I fixed that as soon as I got him home. Let's just say he won't forget last night as long as he lives," she smirked and gave me a wink.

"Stop, I want to be able to forget," I groaned, shaking my head to ward off any images.

"Humph. I'm sorry, Taryn. I really didn't think he was that kind of guy."

"No, I'm the sorry one. I know why he was out last night. It was my fault, he walked in on me and Robert yesterday."

"You went back to Robert?!" Kandice gasped, looking like she might strangle me.

"No, no way. Robert showed up, as usual lately, and I asked him if he ever paid for sex."

Kandice looked confused.

"I'll back up to that part later. He said no, that it was illegal and he wouldn't risk all he had for that. Then I made a comment about adultery being illegal too, and he said not if sex was his gift. So, I basically said his sex wasn't all that great. He immediately knew I was referring to Alex, and that made him mad. So he grabbed me, told me he'd show me awesome, and kissed me, pinning me to the couch. That's when Alex walked in. Alex punched him in the face and left. I haven't seen him since," I explained. I felt miserable.

Kandice put her arms around me. "I'm sorry, and I hate Robert."

"Yeah, me too. It gets worse. I got another threat last night. It was the sharp end of a meat thermometer missing its cord and a lovely note threatening to ice me." I started to cry but wiped my tears away and took a deep breath. "When life gives you lemons, make lemonade right?"

"That's going to be one sour glass of lemonade," Kandice commented.

"Then I guess I'm going to have to find a lot of sugar."

We both laughed. I filled Kandice in on the rest of the events that had happened. Now she understood why I had asked Robert those questions.

"Do you think Robert is involved in the murder in some way?" she asked.

"I don't know. I don't think so," I said.

"He has been acting weird; he has to be up to something," Kandice pointed out.

"Probably, I just don't think it's murder." I couldn't picture Robert as a murderer. He's stupid sometimes but kind. However, I would not have guessed he would trap me on the couch either. No, he couldn't be a murderer; it would be too messy for him.

"So what are you going to do next?" She asked.

"I don't know. I think I'm going to have my locks changed and have them put an extra one on my back door. Then I'll probably go have lunch at my mom's and see how they are doing. I don't really want to stay here alone all day. Plus, it'll keep my mind off what's been going on."

"Or we could spy on Robert," Kandice suggested with a grin that was way too eager. I watched her bounce lightly on the balls of her feet.

"Why? I don't think it's a good idea for me to be within a square mile of Robert if I want to stand a chance with Alex," I replied, trying not to burst her bubble.

"I don't see Alex here trying to make up. From what I saw last night, he's doing his own thing," she sassed back.

"I'm hoping dinner was all it was, and that she is an old friend or client of his, not a date. I don't want to make more mistakes."

"Mistakes are life, girlfriend."

"True. But you're supposed to learn from them."

"And just what are we learning by not following Robert? Nothing, I think we would learn more if we followed him. We'd find out what he's been up to." Kandice expressed.

"You have to be at work in less than an hour, and I have locks to change. Not going to happen, Kandice."

I stood my ground this time.

Chapter 13

An hour later, we were sitting in Kandice's jeep with binoculars, feeling like real-life spies, watching Robert's house. She had gone home to change clothes and came back dressed in black from head to toe. I just wore jeans and a sweater. It was broad daylight; I didn't think the black was necessary. Kandice was on call for the rest of the week for orthodontic emergencies while the doctor was on his yearly cattle round-up trip. All she had to do this morning was check messages and schedule any patients who needed something before he got back. Lucky me. She had no calls this morning, so there was plenty of time to spend sitting in her jeep watching Robert's house.

Robert owned a mansion compared to my condo. It sat on a beautiful forested lot toward the north edge of town. The Winterburn River ran through part of it, leaving him with his own private Colorado beach. Just a little up from the beach, he had a gazebo with glass doors on opposite sides and large glass windows. They could be opened up in the summer to make you feel like you were outside, and closed up for winter to keep you warm and toasty. Inside is a six-person hot tub, a wet bar, and a stone grill. He even has heated walkways, so he doesn't have to shovel snow in the winter just to get to it. The house looked like a large cabin with wrap-around decks and a barn-style roof. It is country but classy. It has a three-car attached garage. He also has beautiful gardens filled with wildflowers surrounding the house.

We were parked slightly up the road on a hill overlooking his place. There is only one country road that runs along the river to his place, so hiding during the day was not easy. Lucky for us, we were behind a large willow that I hoped was blocking his view of us.

"I don't see any movement," I hissed. "We should go back home. I need to call the locksmith. It's after eight now; they should be open.

Kandice heaved a phone book from under her seat and flopped it into my lap.

"Here, call them while I watch the house."

"Gee, thanks." I rolled my eyes and pulled out my phone. After calling several locksmiths, Phil's Lock and Key won the price war. He was the cheapest and could come by this afternoon. Unfortunately for me, that meant our little spy game had plenty of time to continue.

Kandice was leaning forward with her eyes glued to the binoculars when she shouted,

"There he is! He's coming out!" while jabbing me with her finger.

I about jumped out of my seat. We had sat in silence for so long, I didn't expect an outburst like that. I picked up my binoculars and peered through them.

"He has someone with him, but I can't see her face. She has long blond hair."

We sat staring for a few minutes longer. Then the mystery woman turned around. Kandice and I gasped.

"That's Cindy," I said.

At the same time, Kandice said,

"That's the woman I saw Alex with."

"You saw her with Alex?" I asked, and again Kandice asked at the same time, "She's the woman you met yesterday?"

"Yes," we said in unison.

My heart was racing, and my head hurt.

"How do they all know each other? None of this makes sense. I need to think about this for a moment." I threw my arms up in the air after a minute of trying to connect the dots. "I can't think of anything. Nothing ties them together. At least I know she didn't stay with Alex last night. She had Robert for dessert instead."

"That is unless she wanted seconds," Kandice smirked.

"Ew! Not funny!" I grumbled. "I'm going to pretend you didn't just say that."

"Right, sorry. Hey, look, they're leaving," she pointed.

The garage door opened, and his Corvette backed out. Kandice waited until he was a little down the road before she pulled out. This country road doesn't get a lot of traffic. We didn't want him to see us. Once on the highway though, traffic would be busy enough that we could follow them a couple of cars back. I could see him turning left onto the highway. He was headed south. Kandice sped up so we wouldn't lose him as she pulled onto the highway. I could still see them; it looked like they were headed towards Cindy's place. I thought about calling Alex but decided not to. I didn't want to appear too anxious. They turned left onto Cedar Street. I was right; he was taking her home. We pulled into her subdivision and parked a few houses back.

We sat and watched them go inside. Not long after, the door opened, and Robert stepped out, followed by Cindy. She hugged him and kissed him on the cheek. I think she said thank you, but it was hard to tell. I'm not all that good at lip-reading. Robert's back was to us. I couldn't see any expressions or words from him. She turned around and went back inside. Robert got back into his car and pulled away. Kandice and I ducked for cover. He was going to have to drive right past us.

"Did he see us?" I asked.

"I don't think so," Kandice said.

"Good, let's go before anyone gets suspicious."

We followed Robert around for an hour or more while he went to the post office, the hardware store, the bank, and the coffee shop.

"This is boring and pointless," I complained as we sat outside the coffee shop. We were parked one row back in the parking lot, watching Robert drink his coffee.

"We should give it up. We've been sitting in the car all morning and nothing has happened."

"Not nothing," Kandice said. "You found out who's been hanging out with Robert and Alex."

"That just leaves me with more questions. Take me home. I'm done with this."

"Okay," she said with a sigh.

Kandice was about to back out of the parking spot when a tap at the window startled me. I jumped. It was Robert. I rolled my window down a small crack.

"What do you want?" I yelled through the tiny crack.

"How's your morning going? See anything interesting?" He smirked.

"What are you talking about?" I asked. Trying to look confused and innocent at the same time.

"You've been out here in the jeep all morning. I just thought I'd ask if you accomplished anything," he said, grinning.

"I still don't know what you're talking about."

"Here."

He held up two coffees.

"I know you have been following me, and I hope I made it interesting. Then again, it must have been hard for the two of you to sit out here in the cold without coffee. That's why I chose to end up here." His grin was even bigger now. "I must say, I am impressed you lasted this long."

"We don't need coffee, thank you," I said, turning my nose up at him.

"Please, I know you both better than that. Neither one of you can hardly walk past a coffee shop without needing to go inside, let alone sit outside one for thirty minutes. Here, hazelnut mochas for each of you. Think of it as a peace offering."

"The peace treaty committee is still out. Hand over that mocha!" Kandice said, reaching for it like a starving beast.

I rolled the window down the rest of the way. I didn't want to get between Kandice and her coffee. Geez, I thought I was bad. She leaned over me and snatched one of the coffees from his hand.

"You knew we were following you, so you drug us all over town so we could watch you run dinky errands all morning?" I asked as he handed my coffee to me.

"I admit I added some extra stops. Honestly, I thought the coffee shop was the best one. I knew you'd have a hard time waiting at this one," he chuckled.

"You think you know me so well. Then why don't you keep your hands to yourself? I don't want you!" I snapped at him.

"Harsh, Taryn. Harsh. You just don't know what you want yet," he said. "I do know you very well. That's why I intend to win."

"Nice shiner, Robert, how did you get it? Oh wait, I already know. Taryn's new man beat your ass down. Looks like you already lost," Kandice sneered.

Robert glared at Kandice. "I had almost forgotten how much fun you are to have around, Kandice," he growled.

Before she could say anything, I asked him how he knew Cindy.

He rolled his eyes. "Why were you following me?"

"Answer me first."

"She's an old friend and needed my help. Your turn."

"Someone broke into my house again, and you have been very secretive lately, so why not follow you?"

Robert's face went white except for the black eye; it just looked even darker.

"You think it was me who broke into your house? After everything we have been through?" Then his face turned red.

"I don't know. Maybe?" I shrugged.

"That's ridiculous! If I wanted to hurt you, I would have the other night when your last intruder paid a visit. What did you find this time?"

"The meat thermometer and a note." He was silent for a moment. I could not read his face. Was he angry or nervous?

"Well, have fun with that," he said. "I'm going now. Oh, and stop lurking, Taryn; it's not attractive on you. Kandice, next time bring a whip; it might be fun." He spun around and sauntered off.

"Can you believe the nerve of him?" I asked.

"He's right; this would be good with a whip. Well, not for spying, but..."

"Kandice!"

"No, you're right; the jerk is definitely hiding something. Now what?"

"Take me home; this whole thing sucks."

I checked my messages. I had one from my mom and one from Marcy. I'd call my mom later.

I listened to Marcy's. "Hi, Taryn, it's Marcy, just checking in. I assume everything is running smoothly. Any news on the killer? Dan and the guys are out hiking some trail today, so the girls and I are spending the day at the spa. Only three days to go. Hope you find the killer soon." And she hung up. Ah. Well, I hope that explains why Alex didn't answer my call, but I doubted it.

I decided to work on a few upcoming parties I had to plan, and try to forget everything else that was happening in my life. By the time the locksmith came, I had managed to get a few things done, but nothing compared to my usual productivity. Phil, from Phil's Lock and Key, was a short, balding, stub of a man. He had pudgy hands that didn't seem to fit in the workspace around the door. He didn't say much, just introduced himself and went straight to work. I didn't want to stand over him and make him nervous, so I went to the kitchen and pretended to clean it. That way, if he needed me, I was right there.

Phil had finished and left. I felt much safer now. I thought I had better call Alex and let him know the key I gave him wouldn't work now. My stomach turned as the phone rang.

"Hello," followed by a shortness of breath.

"Alex?"

"Yeah." He was still out of breath.

"Hi, it's Taryn. I know you probably don't want to talk to me, but…"

He interrupted me. "I'm not sure what I want to do with you."

I paused for a moment. What do you say to that?

"I, um, just wanted you to know I had my locks changed today, so the key you have won't work."

Another moment of silence.

"I can give you a new one?"

"I'll think about it," he said. "I have to go."

"Okay. Bye."

I hung up the phone and started to cry again. Then I decided to suck it up. I could feel a rush of anger come over me. If he really couldn't decide if I was worth it, then who needed him? I hadn't done anything wrong. Maybe he wasn't the man I thought he was. I decided right there that I was not calling him again.

I was so angry I cleaned the bathtub in a fit of rage. I guess I'm more like my mom than I thought. I don't overrun the house with chemicals, but when I am mad, I do my best cleaning.

After that dirty job, I had calmed down enough that I would be able to relax for the rest of the evening. I called and checked in with my mom, playing the "I'm sorry. I'm really busy with this wedding card". That got me off the hook, at least until Sunday when the wedding would officially be over. Hopefully, by then, my life might be back to normal too.

Kandice showed up with her dog, Fluffy, under her arm.

"What are you doing here?" I asked, letting them in.

"I thought it could be a girl's night. Trey's gone again, and I knew you could use some company and maybe my dog's teeth if there are any unplanned visitors."

"Ha ha," I laughed and scratched Fluffy's head. "Are you gonna eat the big, bad, mean guy, hmm?" Fluffy just wagged his tail. As soon as Kandice put Fluffy down, Giselle came running out.

"Meow." Fluffy was the only animal Giselle truly liked.

Kandice and I drank wine and listened to some Dean Martin while we cooked dinner. French bread, pan-fried chicken, and tortellini with pesto. I may not be Italian, but I sure love pasta. Once we cleaned up the kitchen after dinner, we all piled onto the couch and watched Overboard. It's another one of my favorite movies. One big happy, weird family.

Chapter 14

When I woke up, Giselle, Fluffy, and Kandice were all still asleep. I quietly snuck into the kitchen and started the coffee. Looking around, nothing seemed out of place, no gifts of horror or nasty notes.

I was pouring my cup of coffee when I heard Kandice shuffling around.

"Mmm... coffee. Why aren't we roommates again?" She asked, rubbing her eyes.

"Your nightlife," I chuckled.

"Right, it is hard to be as active as I am with a man-hating roommate."

"I'm not man-hating!"

"Okay, a less active roommate."

"Ha ha ... Here's your coffee."

I teasingly shoved it at her. "You can stay anytime."

"No bad guys this morning?" She took a long sip of the coffee.

"Nope."

"So what's your plan today? Follow Robert, maybe Alex?"

"No. I have to go out to Crystal Lakes. I have band practice."

"Good, I'll check in on the office and come with you. Maybe that creepy butler will give us more clues."

After breakfast, Kandice took Fluffy home and went to check on the office. I told her I would pick her up since we spent the better part of yesterday in her jeep. I dressed in a sweater and jeans, fed my cat, locked my new lock, then headed down to my truck.

I needed gas before going to Crystal Lakes, so I backed out of my garage and drove down my street towards Main. I pulled into the Conoco on Main and 21st Street. I felt like a bag of hot fries, so after inserting my card at the pump, I selected the pay inside option. Hot fries were reserved for road trips and extremely stressful times. Upon opening the door, I saw the broken nose and foot goon. Flame Boy was working one of the registers. Great. I couldn't turn around and run; I needed to pay for my gas and the hot fries.

I skirted around one of the aisles, keeping my head down, trying not to look suspicious either. I located the hot fries, grabbed them, and planned my escape. I figured I'd wait until someone was checking out with Flame Boy, and then I'd run to the other register to check out. At least that guy looked fairly clean-cut, and seeing how I hadn't done him any bodily harm, he probably wouldn't try to kill me.

The plan was all set and ready to roll when my phone went off with the William Tell Overture. Of course, Flame Boy looked up, and our eyes made contact, or should I say his burned holes in me. After that, all hell broke loose. For a guy with a broken foot, he sure leaped over the counter at me with no problem. I hollered $36.97 on pump #4 and a bag of hot fries to the other register guy. Who, by the way, looked very confused. I ran between the aisles trying to keep as much distance between me and Flame Boy as possible. All the while, the phone kept playing the overture. I made another pass by the register, and the guy yelled $39.13. I pulled out two twenties and came around for a third pass, threw the money at him, and yelled, 'Keep the change' as I ran out the door. With hot fries still in hand, I jumped in my truck. I stepped on the gas and could see Flame Boy in my rear-view mirror, standing outside the door, waving his hands and shouting.

I pulled up to Kandice's house a little flustered, but overall feeling pretty good that I had escaped that nimrod once again. Kandice came out and climbed into the truck.

"What happened?"

"What do you mean?"

"The hot fries have Alex written all over them, but your face suggests a new story."

"Fine. I'll tell you." She could see through me like a mom can when a kid takes a cookie. They just know. By the time I had finished, Kandice had a wad of tissues; she was laughing so hard tears were pouring out.

"The overture playing the whole time is the icing on the cake. None of that stuff happens to me," she wheezed.

"Why would you want it to?" I snorted in bewilderment.

"I don't know. It's just so funny."

I guess it was a little funny. I opened my hot fries and stuffed a handful into my mouth. Mmm…

"That's disgusting!" Kandice wrinkled her nose.

"What?" My mouth was still sort of full.

"It's bad enough that those taste like hot cardboard, but then you stuff your mouth like that. Ew."

"Excuse me!" I grabbed a tissue and blew my nose.

"And they make your nose run."

"It's good for the sinuses."

I continued to eat my hot fries. "Besides, those pork skins you eat are horrible. Greasy puffs of fake pig skin."

"At least my nose and eyes don't run like I've got a nasty cold," she argued.

"Fine, let's call a truce. We are both gross."

We pulled into Crystal Lakes. It really was a beautiful place. You felt like a princess coming home to your castle.

"So, Marcy hasn't talked to you much this week?" Kandice asked as she hopped out of the truck.

"I know. So weird. She wouldn't leave me alone all summer, and now nothing. It doesn't seem right. She's a control freak. She should be here making sure everything is the way she wants it to be," I replied as I climbed out myself.

"Maybe she is too busy pampering herself before the wedding."

"I guess. She hasn't come out since the murder. I think she is scared. That's why she asked me to find the murderer."

We walked up to the door, but before I knocked, Sam answered.

"Ladies." and motioned us in.

"Good morning, Sam."

"Miss O'Kelly." His voice was cheery. Not at all cold and creepy like the other day.

I went to the ballroom, and the tables were set up. Marcy had chosen gold tablecloths with red napkins. In the center of each table would be a wreath of yellow, magenta, coral, and lavender roses; red maple leaves and hypericum berries round out the arrangements. In the center of the wreaths, there will be white floating candles in circular vases, which have been painted with golden swirls and gold flecks. The stage was at the far end of the room opposite the door. I would decorate the stage once the band let me know where their stuff needed to be.

The group was a local swing/jazz band called Pack Rats, a clever spin-off from the original Rat Pack. They did a pretty good job of remaking the music too. The group was fairly hard to get since they are in high demand in Silver Springs, but I managed to pull it off. Right on time, the guys came through the door.

"Hi, Taryn O'Kelly." I stuck out my hand. George, a tall, skinny guy with brown hair, introduced himself as the lead singer of the group.

"This is Max, our percussionist; Will, our bassist; and Pete, our saxophonist."

"Nice to meet you all," I said.

They walked over to the stage and began their setup. Max was an average-sized guy with fluffy red hair and a goofy big smile. Will looked like he was the hunk in the band, with dark, almost black hair, and a very muscular body. Pete was the least memorable. His features were plain: brown hair and brown eyes, not skinny but not fat.

They warmed up a bit and rehearsed Marcy's and Dan's song. "New Kind of Love," by Frank Sinatra. They sounded great. I actually wished Marcy was here to hear it. She would be pleased.

Once rehearsal was over, I wrapped the stage in red cloth, making large sweeping sashes. Across the front of the stage, I tied gold bows at the peak of each sash. Once done, I checked to make sure everything was all set. The florists and caterers were ready to roll on Saturday. Two days and counting. Everything on my list was checked off except finding the killer, of course. With nothing more needed, I snatched Kandice and headed back into town.

"What are you going to do now?" Kandice asked.

"Go home and think about this case. I need to list what I know and what I need to find out," I said as I pulled my truck onto the highway.

"I'm coming too," she declared, settling in for the drive.

We pulled up to the house, parked, and went inside. I fixed us mashed potato and roast beef sandwiches and more coffee for lunch.

Mmm... I love mashed potatoes, gravy, and meat, all grilled into a fat, warm sandwich. Just the comfort food I needed, I thought to myself. Kandice didn't mind it either. We ate our lunch quietly, both of us thinking.

Once the dishes were cleaned up, I went to my office and got a notepad. I started listing the things we knew, which didn't feel like much. As I racked my brain for more detail, I remembered the picture I took of the numbers from Cindy's house. I hadn't called them yet. I pulled out my phone and wrote down the numbers.

"What should we do?" I asked Kandice. "I'm not sure what to say that would be believable."

Kandice suggested, "Just say you got this number from your friend, Jessica. Then play it up from there depending on what they say."

"Okay." I picked up the phone and called the number marked "pick-up." I don't know why, but my stomach was in knots. It rang three times, and then an eerie voice answered. One I was pretty sure I had heard before.

"Hello?"

"Hi, I um, I got this number from a friend, and I was wondering if I could pick up the items she had waiting for her?"

"What's the code?" The voice asked. Code? There was a code? Great.

"Code, um she forgot to give me the code," I said.

"No code, no pick-up."

"Oh, okay, I'll ask."

Click, the line was dead.

"That was weird. He hung up on me." I furrowed my eyebrows and looked down at my phone.

"What did he say?" Kandice wanted to know.

"The voice sounded familiar, but I can't think of who it was. He said I needed a pick-up code, whatever that means?"

"Call the other number." She sat on the edge of her seat.

I dialed the second number. It rang six times, no one answered, and there was no way to leave a message. I hung up.

"Now what?" I huffed.

Kandice suggested we look them up on Google. So we went to my office and checked the pick-up number. It said it was registered to an Albert Einstein on County Road 250, Silver Springs, CO. We looked at each other and laughed. If we wanted more exact information; we could join the finding service for a fee. No thanks. We tried to look up Albert Einstein of Silver Springs, but we kept getting stuff on the real Einstein.

We decided to try phone number two. It was a bust too. That number was loosely associated with a nonprofit piano repair company. It looked like the company took donated or run-down pianos, repaired them, and then gave them to orphanages in other countries or other charitable causes. Why would that horrible stripper have a number for a charity? She didn't strike me as someone who would do something for anyone but herself.

I got out the Silver Springs phone book and looked at all the addresses on County Road 250. At first, there was nothing, but as I looked closer, I found an Albert E. Stein located at 1753 County Road 250. Kandice and I looked at each other.

"Could it be the same person?" If so, the address is very close to Crystal Lakes. I said.

"Grab your purse. Let's go," Kandice said.

"No, I don't want to go investigate anymore today. I haven't been on a run in days. I need to clear my head. We can go out in the morning."

Kandice started to protest, but her phone rang. It was Trey. She said a few dirty things and then checked to make sure I would be okay if she didn't come home tonight. I reassured her that I would be fine. Besides, I hoped Alex would come by tonight, and I didn't want Kandice babysitting me anyway.

She hung up and grinned. "Okay, let's go."

I looked at her blank-faced; "I thought you were leaving to hook up with Trey."

"Oh, I am, but not for a couple more hours; plenty of time to check out the new address."

"Ugh..." I sighed, "I want to squeeze a run in. I need to run to clear my head, but what if Alex stops by? I want to be here. Besides, this will just be another wild goose chase I am not in the mood for."

"You won't find the killer sitting at home," Kandice protested. "and Alex will be here waiting for you if he's the man I hope he is."

"Fine. Let's get this over with," I whined as I grabbed my purse and followed Kandice out of the house. We got into Kandice's jeep and drove off. I was annoyed with just about everything in life right then and became very unpleasant company on the 30-minute drive out to the middle of nowhere.

"Taryn, what's the deal? You're cranky."

"I am," I grumbled in a less-than-friendly voice. "I want this whole stupid thing over with!"

"It's not my fault," Kandice snapped back at me. She had a short temper as well.

"No, it's not, but you aren't helping. I told you I wanted to go on a run, not drive around chasing ghosts!"

"I never made you come along; I just wanted to help get this damn investigation over with. The sooner this is done, the sooner you can get back to having a life. So excuse me for being a friend and offering to help out! I am tired of all your excuses for not being happy," Kandice snarled, shooting me a withering glare.

"I don't have any excuses!" I shot back.

"Yes, you do. It's always about work and how busy you are."

"Sorry, I am focused on my work," I said loftily.

"It's not focus, it's delay tactics. You were never going to get over Robert and, unfortunately, now Alex too."

"What are you talking about? I am over Robert, and as for Alex... well... I will be very soon." I wanted to cry.

"Look, Taryn, I didn't mean to hurt your feelings; it's just that you have worked too hard to let a couple of stupid guys and a stripper mess up your life again. I want you to find this creep and bring him down, get Marcy's wedding over with, and move on with your life. You have to admit this has been the most fun we have had together in a long time."

This was true, I thought and smiled. "You're right, and I am sorry. It has been fun. Maybe you should become a private investigator instead of a hygienist since you like spying so much."

"Nah... It's only fun when you're with me," she replied.

We both smiled. Minutes later we were at the address of Albert E. Stein. A long gravel driveway led us to a large, dusty lot with a big metal warehouse in the middle. There were a couple of truck docking bays and steel roller garage doors. It didn't appear to be occupied by anyone. We pulled up to the warehouse, got out of the jeep, and looked around. There were no windows or signs, nothing to identify who or what the warehouse was for. The place looked abandoned. No cars parked out front. Weeds had sprouted up around the base of the building.

We knocked on the door. No one answered. Kandice tried the handle, but the door was locked. We continued to creep around the building. The locks on the garage doors looked new. I tried to guess the combo on one of the locks but was unsuccessful. After about 20 minutes, I started to worry about trespassing charges. Finding nothing, we headed home.

"Well, that was a bust," I said, as I got out of the jeep. "We didn't get any closer to finding the killer."

"I know, maybe tomorrow," she said.

"Thanks for supporting me and helping with this nightmare," I said, closing her Jeep's door.

"No problem!" She said as she pulled away.

I walked up the steps to my house and locked the door behind me. It was 4:30. I needed to change so I could run.

Chapter 15

I dressed in my usual running attire, a pink sports shirt and black shorts. It was getting a little too chilly for just a sports bra. I hit the trail. It felt great. It was cooling off quite a bit with October right around the corner, but the air smelt fresh, and the wind on my cheeks was just what I needed. I ran along, not thinking of the killer, Robert, or Alex. As I was running, I noticed a blond woman sitting by the river reading. I stopped and realized it was Cindy. The book was titled *Girl Don't Be an Idiot*. I walked over to her. "Cindy?" Her eyes were red.

"Oh, hi, Taryn". She greeted with a sniffle.

"You okay?" I asked, shifting my weight.

"Yes, I just thought this book might help me get over Frank."

She closed the book and held it up, showing me.

"Is it working?" I asked.

"No, not really. It's just hard not to see all of our adventures everywhere I look. Silver Springs is too small to hide memories. I'm thinking about moving."

"Have you seen Frank?" I asked, sitting down next to her.

"He came by about an hour ago to get the rest of his stuff. He didn't have much to say. I didn't either."

"I am so sorry. It will get better, trust me. Hey, I saw you yesterday with an old friend of mine. Robert Campbell."

"You know Robert. Isn't he a dream? I'd take him in a second. I could probably forget about Frank too, but he's hung up on some girl that's seeing someone else right now," Cindy said excitedly, clasping her hands together.

"Oh yeah. So, how do you two know each other?" I asked, trying to sound friendly.

"Well, we hooked up one time a few years ago before Frank. I had just moved here from Greenville, South Carolina. He was so nice to me. He even let me stay at his place until I found my own place. He's helped me out a few times when I was in a bind. Once he got engaged, I missed my window of opportunity with him. I think it's the same girl he was supposed to marry that he's hung up on," she sighed.

"Robert is a really sweet guy; always willing to help those in need," I said, trying not to choke on my words.

We sat in silence for a moment. I'm sure both of us were thinking about Robert, although my thoughts were not fond ones.

"The detective had a few more questions for me," Cindy offered, breaking the silence.

"Oh, did they have any more information?" I asked, trying not to sound too eager.

"I met one very attractive detective at Pepe's. He was not one of the ones who had stopped by the house. He asked me to meet him. We were having a drink, and Robert came in. When I saw him, I asked the officer if we were finished. He said if I had nothing more to add, then yes. I went over to Robert and told him what had happened. I didn't want to be alone, so he offered to let me stay with him."

I'm sure he did, I thought. "Yeah, Robert is a nice guy like that. What else did the police want?"

"They had pictures of a couple of men. They wanted me to see if I had seen them around my place with Jessica. I hadn't seen the men before."

"What did they look like?" I asked. I didn't even know the police had suspects.

"Why?" she asked back, furrowing her eyebrows.

"I'm sorry. It's just that they haven't shown me any pictures, and I was Jessica's friend; maybe I have seen the men. If you described them to me, I could let the police know if I have seen them."

Please buy that story, I thought. I crossed my toes hoping.

"Not much to describe; I didn't look at them that long. I knew right away I had never seen them before," she shrugged.

"Do you remember anything?" Please let her think of something, I thought to myself. I hope she doesn't think I'm too pushy.

"Well, one had a big scar on his face, and the other looked pale and thin with reddish hair. Sorry, I don't have better descriptions."

"That's plenty. I think I might know who the scarred guy is. I need to go to the police station and let them know. Well, I gotta run. Good luck with everything, Cindy." Before she could say more, I got up and ran off.

I called Detective Parker's cell when I got home. I got his voicemail.

"Hi Officer Parker, I saw Cindy on the river walk today, and she described someone I might know; a man with a scar on his face. I should be home all evening; please stop by or call. I could tell you where to find him." When I hung up, I felt very pleased with myself.

I started thinking more about what Cindy had said about Robert. If they were together just before we were engaged, he had to have cheated on me with her too. I can't believe he hid her from me while she stayed at his house. I should have read the book, *Girl Don't Be an Idiot*. I can't believe I didn't see any signs. Talk about rose-colored glasses. I was starting to get mad all over again when I thought about something else, Cindy said. She met a handsome officer at

Pepe's. That had to have been Alex, but he's not an officer. Kandice said that's where she saw them. He's up to something. At least I know now that he didn't do anything with her, even if I don't know what he's been up to.

I heard someone coming up the steps. I went to my office window and saw that it was Detective David Parker. I hurried to the door and opened it.

"Hello, Detective," I smiled, calling out to him in a friendly manner.

"Miss O'Kelly, you have information on these guys?" He pulled out two pictures. It was Scar Face and Flame Boy, the goons from Happy Trails Trailer Park.

"I sure do. I can even tell you where they live."

David's facial expression said he was not surprised.

"How do you know them?" he asked in an exasperated tone.

"Well... I've run into them once or twice before," I replied vaguely.

"Why do I get the feeling that's not all that happened?" he grumbled, shaking his head with a sigh.

"Okay. I'll tell you, but you have to promise not to take me to jail. Or laugh. Or tell Alex."

I was not about to get busted while helping him with his case.

"Miss O'Kelly, I can't promise any of those things. What did you do?" He demanded, becoming impatient. He crossed his arms with a light scowl.

"Well... I sort of kicked Scarface in the groin with my three-inch heels and then ran over his buddy, Flame Boy," I said sheepishly. I grinned, hoping to stay out of trouble.

"What?" he exclaimed.

"Well, he was trying to make me pay this really nasty fat guy named Billy for Jessica's back rent payment. He grabbed me and said I'd be a fun time and could work off her debt."

I spoke quickly in order to defend myself.

"Why didn't you report this?" he huffed. He looked more stressed with me than usual.

"Well, I've never hit-and-run anybody before, and I wasn't sure what exactly my report would fall under. So... I left it alone."

"Okay." He said hesitantly, "Did you have something to do with the bar fight the other night then too?"

"Um? What do you mean?" I tried to sound innocent.

"We had a call about a bar fight at Joe's, and now that I think about it, Bobby Dirken's description of the girl who started it all matches yours. I would never have guessed it to be you until now."

"Well, that wasn't my fault either!" I protested, throwing my hands up in defense.

"Of course not, Miss O'Kelly, so what did happen?" He groaned.

"Well, I was out with my friend, Kandice." I wasn't about to tell him I was spying on Alex; my hole was deep enough. "And Flame Boy, the one I ran over, and his posse of hoodlums came in as Kandice and I were leaving. Flame Boy grabbed my hair and told me Billy wanted his money. So before I could escape, my friend punched him in the face, breaking his nose and sending him into the crowd. We narrowly escaped."

"Amusing as this all is, Miss O'Kelly, this group of hoodlums, as you call them, are very dangerous. Making them mad at you is not a good idea," he warned.

I nodded. I made a show of taking him very seriously before asking with a grin.

"Soooo, who's worse, Scar Face or Flame Boy?"

"Why?" he asked, scowling again.

"Just curious?"

"Curiosity is not a good thing for you. It's what got you into this mess in the first place. Richard and Bobby Dirken are not people to be messed with," he emphasized.

"They seem like idiots to me."

"They have served time in the state penitentiary, and it's only a matter of time before we send them back. Bobby, the one you call Flame Boy, does most of Richard's dirty work, but if Richard feels his little brother isn't getting things tied up fast enough, he will move in and take over the job."

"So am I going to jail now?"

"No, off the record, those two deserved what you did to them, but mostly I'm just glad you're safe. They are terrible people. So the only connection that you know of between the Dirkens and Jessica is this Billy's rent money?"

Just like a switch, he went from sweet and caring to big bad detective pants. Sheesh.

"Yes, Detective Parker, that's the only reason I know these guys. They live at Happy Trails Trailer Park."

"I know that, Miss O'Kelly, and you're sure there isn't anything else you know that you haven't shared with me?" he asked skeptically.

"No, she just owed that Billy rent, and the Dirkens want it out of me now. That's it."

"Okay, then, Miss O'Kelly. Have a good night." He nodded and trotted back to his patrol car.

After Detective Parker left, I didn't feel like cooking dinner, so I decided to order pizza. I put up the food I had gotten out to cook. As I waited for my pizza, I kept hearing Albert Einstein's voice. No code. No pick-up. I paced the floor until my doorbell rang. Where have I heard that voice before? I opened the door for the pizza guy. Oh crap!

"Um, hi." I tried to sound cheery. The pizza guy was Richard Dirken, aka Scarface. Really, what are the odds? I hoped he didn't recognize me. Nope, too late, he knew. His eyes bugged out of his head with recognition. His face turned bright red.

"You!" He pulled a gun out of his waistband and leveled it at me.

I went to grab mine, but forgot I had already dressed in my pajamas. It was in my bedroom.

"You're not going to shoot me. You'd never get away in time. You'll be back in prison before I'd have time to come back and haunt you," I sneered. I felt surprisingly brave with a gun in my face.

"You're right, I'm not going to shoot you, at least not yet," he growled. "You are coming with me."

"No, I'm not," I growled back.

I tried to close the door, but he was faster and blocked it; grabbing me. I started kicking and scratching at him. He suddenly let go as I lunged at him. He stepped to the side, and I tumbled down the steps, landing hard on the sidewalk. Oooh. I groaned. My ankle and head ached with horrible pain. I could feel blood rolling down my cheek. I tried to get up before Richard could get to me, but he was fast and silent. I felt something stab my thigh, and then he picked me up and shoved me into the car.

Everything hurt. Oh God, please get me out of this. Please let one of my neighbors see this. I prayed. Where's Robert or Alex when I needed them? I tried to stay awake, but my head throbbed. I must have passed out because the next thing I knew, I was handcuffed to a bed. My ankle had been wrapped, and I had a bandage on the right side of my forehead. I had scrapes and bruises all over. My ankle throbbed with pain, and I was pretty sure it was broken. I felt like I had been drugged.

"I warned you to stay out of this, Miss O'Kelly. I gave you plenty of chances, but you just couldn't listen, could you?"

"Who's there?" I demanded. It was the same voice from the phone.

"I think you know," he replied.

A tall, thin, ghostly pale man dressed in a black suit stepped out of the shadows. My eyes widened. It was Sam.

Chapter 16

"You spray painted my beautiful patio; you left the notes and thermometer? Why are you doing this? Detective Parker will catch you." I tugged on the handcuffs. I was still in shock from all that had occurred in the last few hours.

"Miss O'Kelly, they haven't caught me yet. Why do you think I have those two buffoons working for me? They will be caught, not me. Oh, and your Robert, of course. His drunken man-whore state played into my plan perfectly. When the police figure out that he was tricked into paying for sex, they will assume that he became angry and killed her. We have all seen his temper. Since he has a key to your house, naturally they will think he's the one who kidnapped you too," Sam replied. He moved silently across the concrete floor. He paused a couple of feet from me and simply peered at me with cold, dark eyes.

"He doesn't have a key to my place, and he would never pay for sex. So your plan won't work," I replied.

He chuckled and shook his head. "Oh, but he does, and he did."

"What proof do you have?"

"I have pictures of him entering your home, and I am sure the police do too. If they don't, I have already put together a care package for them. Anonymously, of course."

Oh God. I thought to myself. He had taken my key from the hook. That's how he was always able to just show up. Oh, Robert, how could you be so stupid?

"Even if he did take my key, he wouldn't pay for sex. He never does; women just want him. Jessica would be no different," I argued, not taking my eyes off Sam.

"You see, Miss O'Kelly, I have done my research. Your man, Robert, has an addiction. He wrote a large check to Jessica that night."

"He would never do that," I growled at him.

"He did. She was ready to sign it over to me, before I strangled her, as partial payment on the enormous debt she owed me. She begged me to give her more time. But her time was up."

He had a devilish grin on his face.

"Well, how come the police don't know about the check?" I snapped back, waving my one free hand.

"They do, they have it. I was going to keep the money, but felt that it would better serve me if

I placed it among Jessica's things for the police to find."

How could I have missed so much? I thought. I can't believe Robert paid her anything. Why did Jessica owe him so much money? I was bewildered and wanted to cry. If the police really thought it was Robert, they would never find me before Sam went unhinged on me too.

"I know it's a lot to process, Miss O'Kelly, but I wouldn't worry about Robert too much. Clearly, he wasn't always honest with you either."

"What do you want with me? Why did you bandage me up if you're only going to kill me?" Tears were forming in my eyes. I blinked, trying to stay strong.

"I have plans for you," he said as he stepped closer to me. He ran his hands through my hair. I tried to kick him, but he grabbed my leg.

"Don't fight me, Taryn. Some lords will pay handsomely for a woman of your beauty and energy. Then maybe I could make up some of the money that whore lost me. She was not the kind of woman you are." He cupped my cheek in his rough hand, patting me like a dog. "You are like a wild horse that needs to be broken," he said, leaning closer to my face. He had my hand trapped. "Rest well, Miss O'Kelly, you need to regain your strength," he whispered, grabbing a chunk of my hair, wrenching my head backwards and kissing me.

I spat as he pulled away, screaming, "You'll never get away with this!"

He moved silently across the room as if he were floating, and was gone.

My eyes welled up, and a tear ran down my cheek. Oh God, please let Detective David find me. I started to cry hard. I didn't want to be so weak. Taking a long, deep breath and fanning my eyes, I stopped crying. I need to be brave. I need to think. He won't sell me looking like this, so I have some time.

There was no way to tell what time it was because the room I was in had no windows. The house or whatever I was in was deathly quiet for what seemed like hours. I strained to hear anything; not even the sound of a road could be heard. The only sound I heard was my stomach; it growled, and I was starving. Sitting in silence for what seemed like forever, I finally heard footsteps.

"Hello?" I called. "Is anybody there?" A bead of sweat ran across my forehead, and I began to tremble. Being handcuffed to a bed in a dark room was very frightening. I hated being such a wuss.

Sam entered the room again, holding a box of pizza. "Miss O'Kelly, your dinner. I know you like pizza; I never could have planned your abduction so brilliantly."

"What are you talking about?" I snapped; the anger and rage were building again. The hate I was feeling made me feel as though my hair was about the catch fire.

"You wouldn't listen, warning after warning," he sighed. "So, I admit I thought about killing you at your house. However, that would just bring more investigation. After you ordered pizza, and Richard recognized you, the plan changed. The smartest thing he has done so far was to take you and contact me for a drop-off point," Sam explained.

He carried the pizza box to the bed and opened it up. It was just plain pepperoni.

"And what part of me missing altogether won't bring more investigation?" I asked in a snarky tone. "You're delusional! There is no way the Dirkins won't rat you out! Someone had to have seen him kidnap me. It's only a matter of time before the police show up. Your games don't scare me."

I sat up smugly, feeling pleased with myself. I lied about being scared; I was terrified. Before I could register what was going on; the back of Sam's hand lashed across my right cheek.

"What the hell!" I screamed, tears welling up behind my eyes. I held my stinging cheek with my un-cuffed hand. "I thought I needed to be in better shape to be sold." Sam's eyes were black as coal, and his heart probably was too; the anger streaked across his face. I felt like I was looking at the spawn of Satan.

"You need to know when to shut your mouth!" he growled. "That was a lesson; I should hope you learn it. Where you are going, you get a lot more than a slap in the face for such disrespect."

He threw the pizza at me and stalked out, slamming the door.

My head ached from my additional injury, and I burst into tears. I ate my pizza and cried myself to sleep.

Chapter 17

Alex came by Taryn's house Thursday night with flowers to make amends only to discover Taryn wasn't home. He left a note on the door and hoped she would call him back soon. He headed to his car, replaying the week's events in his mind. Distracted by his own thoughts, he tapped his thumbs on the steering wheel. Feeling a surge of worry and slight jealousy, he realized she could be with Robert. He started his car; the engine roared to life, and he headed to Robert's.

Alex knocked on Robert's door. After a few seconds, Robert answered the door. He was only wearing a pair of black silk boxers, his hair was a tossed mess, and he had a glass of wine in his hand.

"Alex, what brings you here?" he asked in a disgusted tone.

"I'm not happy to see you either," Alex replied coolly.

And he wasn't, especially seeing Robert's lack of clothing. He hoped Taryn wasn't there.

"I have come looking for Taryn," he admitted, crossing his arms. He could not believe he was even speaking to this moron.

Seeing the concern in Alex's eyes, brought a smile to Robert's face. He knew that at least this time, he had won.

"Why would I tell you if she is here? She is free to choose whomever she wants, and by my calculations, it won't be long until I have her," he smirked, placing one hand on the door and taking a sip of wine. He started to close the door, but Alex put his foot in the way.

"She is free to choose whomever she wants," he growled, "but I need to speak to her first."

"Well, unfortunately for both of us, she is not here, and I have guests to entertain. Good night." He shoved Alex out and shut the door in his face. Robert grinned with delight, pleased with himself and very happy to know that they were still fighting.

Alex groaned with frustration. Robert practically begged for an ass-whooping every time he opened his mouth. He sighed heavily, deciding she must be out with her friends or family. He strode back to his car; he would not bother her tonight. He would see her tomorrow. Tomorrow night was the rehearsal dinner, and he had a case to help solve. Two very important jobs he hoped would soon be over. Then, if it was possible, he would repair his relationship with Taryn.

He called David Parker and asked if they could meet to go over the case again. Something was nagging at him, and he needed to find out what it was.

Once at David's house, the men made a pot of coffee and spread the case across David's table.

"You really care about her, don't you?" David asked. "She is cute but slightly annoying."

"She's not annoying, she's ambitious, and she takes her job seriously just like us," Alex protested a bit. "She thinks she's helping."

"Her job isn't a private investigator like you or a detective like me. Her job is to plan parties. She needs to stay out of this. Now she is a target," David snorted, while sorting the evidence in chronological order.

"I agree, but she feels like she has to get this cleared up before the wedding so her client can be happy. I can't blame her for that," Alex replied, folding his hands and furrowing his brows in concentration.

"No, but she is making a mess of things. You were right not to tell her that this is your case too."

"I wonder if that's true. I wanted to protect her, not lie to her. And to answer your earlier question, yes, I do care about her, probably more than anyone."

"Then let's catch this asshole, so we can all sleep better," replied David.

"What's your feeling about Robert? The pieces don't quite add up; there is something off about him, something I don't like." Alex said, looking over the evidence against him.

"If you want my opinion," David said, "I think he's a spoiled jerk who typically gets what he wants. I think he is mostly harmless and obsessed with Taryn. He hates that you are in her life because she's probably the first thing he can't have, as long as you're in the picture. I don't think he did it."

"If he didn't do it, then why is he sneaking around?"

"My guess is when you write a check for $1,500 to a stripper that ends up dead, you have to cover your ass." David rolled his eyes.

"He did," Alex said, "with the note he and Jessica signed explicitly saying it was not dirty money, just a gift. This brings me to another question: who gives a $1,500 gift to a stripper they just met? Strippers make good money, better than what we bring in."

"Indeed, it makes no sense, but the contract he provided looks authentic, and our guys said her signature matched that of her probation papers. It doesn't appear to have been forced; it's legit," David said. He picked up the piece of paper and handed it to Alex, who took it, examined it briefly, and discarded it on the table again.

"What did you get out of that Cindy character the other night?" David asked, moving to the next name on the list.

"Not much, the same as your crew. Jessica was a horrible roommate, owed her money, slept with her boyfriend, and never helped around the house. She admitted she wanted to kill Jessica that night once she found out she had seduced her boyfriend. Cindy said it was just how she felt at the time and would never have truly acted on it. She was going to kick her out once she arrived home. She did not know where Jessica's gig was; just that she was on one. Cindy knows Robert, which makes me suspicious. He showed up during our meeting. I asked how she knew him, and she said that Robert was a close friend and he had helped her out a few times over the years. She went home with him after our meeting ended."

"I still think Robert is just a playboy with more money to burn than he knows what to do with," David said. "He inserts himself whenever a beautiful woman is in distress."

They pushed the evidence against Robert aside and pulled out the crime scene photos, including all the warnings Taryn had gotten.

"I checked the handwriting on the notes to Taryn, and there is no match to Robert's letter. So if he did write them, he had someone else do it," David said. He spread the photos out over the table.

"Did your guys check the notes against the Dirken's?" Alex asked.

"Yes, we did, and still no match," David sighed.

"Who do we have left?" Alex asked.

"Billy Martin, the guy Jessica owed rent money to, Samual Thompson and Betty Williams. Samual and Betty are the only other two that would have access to the Crystal Lakes Property," David replied, rubbing his temples. "Apparently, Jessica owed a lot of people money. The strange thing is we found $10,000 taped up under her bed at Cindy's. That plus Robert's check is $11,500. That's quite a bit of cash lying around for someone so desperate for money," David pointed out.

"When we arrested her in Denver for drug dealing, she said she had never dealt drugs before. The amount she had on her was minimal. She said she didn't know who she had gotten the drugs from, just that the pick-up location was in a brick wall next to the industrial park. We went and found the loose bricks where drugs could be stashed, but never did find the handler. I surveilled the area for weeks but never could get a lead. My guess is that the handler was breathing down her throat for ratting the location out, and possibly disposing of the drugs to not get caught," Alex said, leaning back in his chair.

"Hmm," David said, rubbing his chin. "I am going to call the PD and get a list of all known residents with any form of a drug background. We can then reference it with all the information we currently have and see if we can find a common thread. I also have guys looking into the piano repair company/charity the phone number was connected to. We should have more information by morning."

"Good, we also need writing samples from Samual, Betty, and Billy. I will get Sam and Betty first thing in the morning," said Alex.

"I will visit Billy then too," David replied.

They continued poring over the information until the late hours of the night.

Sam stormed into the tiny cold room where I lay on the bed, still handcuffed, slamming the door behind him and startling me awake.

"You didn't tell me you were dating the damn private investigator that helped arrest Jessica!" he shouted, his face turning red with rage. "You set this up! What have you told him?"

He grabbed my arms, squeezing so tightly that I was afraid he might break them. I was thoroughly confused. Had he lost his marbles? I tried to kick at him, but my ankle was still throbbing.

"What are you talking about?" I grimaced with pain.

"Your boyfriend came by today with a warrant asking for a sample of my handwriting, what do you know?!" He shook me harder.

"Nothing, I swear. Who are you talking about?" I yelped. I was confused and in a lot of pain. What the hell was going on?

"ALEX!" he bellowed.

"Alex? He is a pilot, not a private investigator," I argued.

"And Jessica! What about her?" He snarled.

"We hired her through an agency; believe me, I have never met her before."

I struggled in his grip. His hands were cold and vice-like.

He let go of his grip, started to step back, and as smooth and quick as a cat, he backhanded me across the face. A small trickle of blood poured out the side of my mouth.

"You really are dumb," he said with a smile. "It looks to me that all the men in your life lie to you. Never mind, my plan will still go through, and you will be gone by tomorrow."

"I thought I needed to get better first?" I needed to buy myself some time.

"I won't make as much money off of you in this condition, but it will have to do. I hope you're not claustrophobic; you have a long, tight journey." He smiled again and left.

Once again, I started to cry. I was beginning to wonder what in my life was true. Alex is a P.I.? Why wouldn't he have told me? Did he know Jessica? Did she know him? When he picked her out, he seemed adamant she was the one he wanted, to the point that I was annoyed. When we met her, she didn't seem to know him, although she seemed to want to hook up with him. If he helped put her in jail, wouldn't she want to stay away from him? Okay, now I am more confused than ever. I was going to figure this out. It's just a puzzle; put it together. The claustrophobia clued me in. Sam was a drug handler, Jessica lost his money somehow, and I was to be shipped inside a piano, to God knows where, to become a sex slave. I really hope Alex is good at the job he conveniently forgot to tell me about, or else I wouldn't see anyone I cared about again.

Some time passed, and Sam came back whistling with delight and carrying what looked to be lunch. Great, more pizza.

"Here, eat!" he demanded. "You have a long trip ahead of you; I have made all the arrangements. You leave shortly."

"I am not going!" I shouted at Sam.

"You don't have a choice," he smiled.

"So, Sam, how long have you been drug-running with pianos?" I asked with a smug smile. I had to buy time.

His face was turning bright red again. I struck a nerve. Yes, that means I was on to something. I took a bite of my pizza and waited for his answer.

"It's brilliant actually; the piano company is owned by an alias of mine."

"Albert E. Stein," I blurted out.

He glared at me. "How do you know that name?"

"Jessica had a big mouth," I smiled, proud of myself.

"It doesn't matter. Albert E. Stein has no connection to me. It's as though he is a real person. They'll never tie him to me, and you'll never be able to tell."

His devilish grin widened as recognition spread across my face. Oh crap, he had drugged me again. I tried to fight it, but the room was going black.

"Sleep well, Miss O'Kelly. I hope you like Columbia."

Chapter 18

The rehearsal dinner was to start in a few hours; no one had heard from or seen Taryn. Kandice had called Alex, freaked out that the murderer had her. They met at the police station.

"Alex, how could you be such an ass!" Kandice screamed. "She cared about you. You were supposed to protect her, and instead, you ran off and pouted like a baby. Why weren't you with her?"

She started to cry. Kandice was always tough, but not this time. She knew something bad had happened to her best friend. She could feel it. Alex placed a comforting hand on her shoulder.

"I messed up. You are right, I should have been with her." Kandice pulled away and smacked him.

Alex, not wavering a bit, said, "I need to tell you something. I am a private investigator and have been working on this case for months. I did not leave to pout; I left to find the killer."

"Why didn't you tell her? She would have left all of this to you."

"At the time, I thought it would keep her safer," he admitted. He felt incredibly dumb in hindsight.

"Well, we can see how that worked out. She's gone!" Kandice screamed again, waving her hands in the air.

"We have arrested Robert for her kidnapping. We have photos of him entering the house on several occasions," Alex said, leaning against the table in the conference room they had met in.

"What has he said?" Kandice asked in a quiet voice.

"Nothing so far; he denies knowing where she is."

"Then you don't have the right guy. I hate Robert, but he would not hurt Taryn, at least not this way," she calmly said, before shouting, "YOU MUST FIND HER!"

"Kandice, you have to control yourself. We are working on it." Alex moved towards her and placed both hands on her shoulders. "Believe me, I care a lot about her too. I will find her. I need you to run the rehearsal dinner in her place. I don't want to spook anybody, especially the killer. She is at home very sick; that is all anybody needs to know. Do you understand me?"

"Yes, but you have taken Robert into custody; does this mean it was or wasn't him?" Kandice demanded, pushing Alex away.

"I don't know what to believe just yet, but I have a feeling that if it isn't Robert, this will make the killer cocky and hopefully trip him or her up. Just run the dinner, please. I will be there 10 min before it starts. Just act normal," Alex pleaded with her. He needed time to catch the killer off guard.

Kandice took a deep breath. "Let me talk to Robert first, and then I will do as you ask." She crossed her arms as if no was not an answer she would accept.

Alex looked annoyed but reluctantly said yes.

Kandice walked very calmly into the holding room where Robert sat. She was escorted by two uniformed police officers. He looked sick, pale, and a mess.

"Robert," Kandice asked in a curt voice, "where is Taryn?"

"I don't know. If I did, believe me, I would tell you. I want to know what happened to her just as much as you do. If anything happens to her I will never forgive myself." Robert looked like he might cry. Something no one had ever seen Robert do.

"I don't believe much of what you say, but if there was ever a time to tell the truth, it would be now, Robert," Kandice calmly replied, praying for an answer she could accept.

"I am telling the truth. I don't know where she is, and I did not commit the murder. You have to believe me. I need you to get me out of here. I need to help find her. Every minute I'm stuck in here is a minute wasted on finding her!" He shouted.

"I don't know why, but I believe you. However, I cannot get you out. Hopefully, your being in here is the best plan," Kandice replied. She reluctantly turned to leave as Robert pleaded for his release. The two officers closed the door behind her.

"Alex, I don't believe he did any of it," Kandice said, once outside. "You have the wrong man, and you need to fix this."

"I am trying. Is there anything that the two of you found while doing your own investigation? Anything that might help?"

"This guy with flames on his arms tried to grab her at Joe's Bar and Grill a few nights ago. I had to break his nose just to get him to let her go. The same guy chased her around Conoco a couple of days ago. She barely got away."

Alex's face was blank, then it turned to shock. "What? Why didn't I hear about any of this sooner?"

Kandice ignored his comment and continued her story. "We followed Robert around all morning two mornings ago, but found nothing except that you must not have slept with that blond thing you were out with the other night."

This time, Alex's face was a mix of anger and confusion. What kind of circus had this become, he thought? "You followed me?"

"No, I was out with Trey and saw you with that woman. So, like any good friend, I let Taryn know about your secret meeting. Which, by the way, was the night Taryn had another threatening visitor. Had you been around, she wouldn't be missing," Kandice said in a very snarky voice. She continued, not letting him get in a rebuttal. "We went to an abandoned warehouse yesterday afternoon." As she said it, her eyes grew wide. "Maybe that's where she is? Of course, a warehouse, it would be like that if this were a movie."

Alex looked shocked and annoyed. This really was a circus. "We are not in a movie! Tell me how to get there."

Kandice explained the route to the warehouse while Alex wrote it down.

"Okay, got it. It's close to Crystal Lakes. I will be at the rehearsal at 10 minutes 'til 5:00. Remember, no one must know Taryn is missing." He turned to run and hollered back, "Call me if you think of anything else."

Alex got into his silver Volkswagen Tiguan and headed straight to the warehouse Kandice had told him about. Traffic in Silver Springs was busy for a Friday afternoon. Alex maneuvered through the downtown chaos until he hit the highway leading out of town. As traffic thinned out, he stomped the gas pedal. If Taryn was at this warehouse, she probably wouldn't be for long. She had already been missing for nearly 24 hours.

David was questioning the Dirkens as Alex drove. He wanted to be there, but he wanted to find Taryn more. David would call if any leads came up. He was certain of that. Alex turned off the highway onto County Road 250. As he motored down the road, a large semi-truck roared past. Alex's stomach lurched as the truck drove by. Something about the truck didn't feel right. He flipped the car around and tailed the truck.

"Dispatch, this is Alexander Cruz, I need the officers at a warehouse on County Road 250, address 1753, immediately to investigate a kidnapping. And get Detective David Parker on the line!" Alex barked into his cell phone as he maneuvered through traffic and kept eyes on the semi.

"Hold on a minute, honey," the dispatch lady said with a croaky smoker's voice. The line played annoying elevator music, adding to Alex's irritation. The line clicked, and David's voice came over. "Alex, it's David. What do you know?"

"David, I am following a truck that I think came from the warehouse. His driver's side tail light is out. I need him pulled over. I have a feeling Taryn is in that truck. We are headed south on Highway 550."

"I'm on my way," David replied. "By the way, the Dirkens have alibis. They both were working last night when Taryn went missing. One at the Conoco and one at Pizza Hut. I am holding them while we check it out. I have Officer Ballenger reviewing the surveillance footage from the Conoco, and Adams is looking into all the deliveries made from Pizza Hut that night."

Sirens blared as the cop cars raced up beside Alex's car. The trucker pulled over. Both men hurled themselves out of their cars. Trying to regain composure, Detective Parker and Alexander Cruz approached the truck driver. Alex stood quietly while David handled the interrogation.

"License and registration," David asked. The man looked like an MMA fighter, beefy and huge, clean-cut.

"Yes, sir. Here, sir." He handed it out the window. The license read Jake Sitton, address Denver, CO. The truck was registered to Sitton Trucking Company.

"Sit tight, I'll be right back." David ran the plates and license. Everything was clean.

"Do you know why I pulled you over, Jake?"

"No, sir," he replied.

"Your driver-side taillight is out. What's the cargo today?" David asked, playing it off as casual conversation.

"Pianos, sir," Jake said.

"Do you mind if I take a look?"

"Here's the paperwork," he said, as he handed it to David.

"It says here you're headed to Mexico," David said, tapping the paperwork.

"The trailer is, sir; I am just taking it to Las Cruces. An international trucking company will take over from there."

"Jake, I am working on a case with a missing person. Would you be willing to let me check the cargo?"

"I was there when they loaded the pianos, sir, and I have a schedule to keep." Jake shifted in his seat. "If I'm not in Las Cruces by tomorrow night, I'll lose the bid and be out the money for the trip."

"I can get a warrant. The piano company you are working this run for is being investigated for a homicide. It won't be hard to get, but it would take longer," David explained, hoping he would not have to go that route.

"Okay, check the load," Jake said, looking frustrated. Jake got out of the truck. He looked like the Hulk. He walked to the back of the trailer and wrenched open the door. "There you see just pianos," he huffed, clearly irritated.

The trailer was packed with pianos tightly wrapped in moving blankets and tape. Nothing seemed out of the ordinary. Detective Parker's phone started buzzing.

"Excuse me a minute," he said. "I need to take this call. Alex, have a look, would you?"

Alex climbed up into the trailer. There was barely enough room to squeeze through the first two pianos; after that, he would have to climb on them to look around. His job was looking for details, but today it seemed like he was bound to fail. He climbed across row after row of pianos. Praying a clue was there. Each piano appeared to be perfectly packed. Everything looked good. With a sunken heart, he started to climb out when he noticed that the top of one of the pianos didn't feel solid. It felt like a metal screen. His fear grew as he reached for his knife to cut the tape off. If Taryn was in here, she would be in bad shape. She was small, but small enough to be in a piano? He cut through the layers of tape and blanket. Usually, he cared about other people's property, but not today. If Taryn wasn't here, he would buy them a new blanket. He pulled back the blanket and saw he was right; a metal screen had been nailed to the top of the piano. He could see auburn hair and an arm through the screen.

"David, call an ambulance, we have a body!" Alex yelled. He pulled his Leatherman out of his pocket and started pulling at the nails holding the screen. The anger inside him pushed out the fear as it grew. Enraged, he ripped part of the screen back with his bare hands and reached in to hold the victim's hand. It was Taryn.

Chapter 19

The guests had started arriving. It was 4:30, and Kandice had heard nothing. Sam and Mrs. Williams had already asked about Taryn. Kandice explained that she was home very sick. Sam replied, "The poor thing is working too hard, planning a wedding, and investigating a murder. When does she have time to sleep?"

"Investigating a murder?" Mrs. Williams gasped.

"Well..." Kandice paused. "She told the bride she would help get this murder thing out of the way. She wasn't really doing all that much. It was just to help the nerves of the bride, you know."

"I will make a batch of my famous healing tea and send it with you tonight. I bet she'll be feeling good as new tomorrow when she drinks it," Mrs. Williams said, snapping her fingers.

"That's very nice of you, Mrs. Williams. I hope you are right." Kandice didn't know if she could keep up this lie. She wanted to cry. Mrs. William had no idea that no amount of tea was going to help Taryn right now. She hoped Alex would call soon.

Guests continued to arrive. Most didn't know Taryn, so they didn't know that things weren't running quite right. Kandice took this as a blessing.

"Where is Taryn?" A shrill voice screeched. The voice came from around the corner. It belonged to none other than the bride, Marcy.

"Where is Taryn, Kandice? I am paying her a lot of money for this wedding, and she isn't even here to make it run smoothly. We have a killer on the loose, the caterer is here but needs direction, and."

Marcy was cut off when Kandice interjected quickly to maintain the peace and story. "She has everything set up, and it's running perfectly. She just isn't here for you to boss around."

"I am going to demand a refund if she is not here in ten minutes," Marcy snarled.

"Oh, shut up, Marcy!" Kandice snapped in a stern but low voice. "You aren't paying for this wedding. My cousin is you spoiled brat."

"It's about to be my money too. So yes, I am paying for this," she snapped back.

"You have no idea what Taryn has done for you. You should pay her double." Kandice could feel her blood starting to boil.

"If she has done so much for me, where is she?" Marcy growled.

"Home very sick because of you!" Kandice could feel tears trying to push forward, but she held them back.

"Tell her to take a DayQuil and get here!" Marcy said, storming off.

Kandice went to the kitchen, where Culinary Crafts, the caters, had set up. A woman with black hair slicked back into a ponytail and dressed in a white blouse, black skirt, and a white apron tied perfectly around her tiny waist came up to Kandice.

"Hi," she said, sticking her hand out. "I am Susan. Where is Taryn?"

"She is at home, sick; I am her assistant, Kandice."

"Taryn left us very detailed orders. However, the bride seems to feel that dinner in the cinema room is unacceptable. Our only other option would be in the dining hall, but it is set up for tomorrow's event," Susan explained with an apologetic expression.

"Did she say why the room is unacceptable?"

"No, I am sorry."

"Okay. Hang tight. I'll go figure this out," Kandice said with a sigh. Kandice headed off to find the real-life Bridezilla.

"Marcy, I need to talk to you," Kandice said through the door to the bridal suite.

"About what? I am getting ready," Marcy answered.

"Dinner in the cinema room." Kandice felt like banging her head against the door instead.

"I already told Susan that was unacceptable," Marcy replied.

"Why not, Marcy?" Kandice said as she shoved her way through the door.

"Get out! How rude!" Marcy shouted. She was sitting on the bed, brushing her hair. "I don't want dinner served in the room that stripper was in."

"The room has been cleaned and set up for a very elegant rehearsal dinner. No one knows there was a stripper in there!" Kandice argued, leaning against the door.

"Except all of the groomsmen!" Marcy snapped.

"So what? Your groom was very faithful. The way I heard it, Alex was the stripper's target, anyway. The way you are behaving, Dan should have had fun with the stripper. You're acting like a spoiled brat. You okayed the dinner in that room and it has been set up. It's final or I'll go talk to Dan," Kandice said in a firm tone. It was like dealing with a child.

"Dan will side with me; he always does." Marcy said slyly.

"Fine. Let's go get him." Kandice turned to leave but stopped when Marcy shouted, "NO! Leave him be. Dinner can be served as planned." she sighed.

"I thought he always sided with you?" Kandice replied snarkily.

"He does, and all I have to do is tell him, but I am bored with this now, so go away."

She waved her hand and went back to brushing her hair. "I like Taryn much better than you. You are hideously rude."

"Taryn has to be nice; you're paying her. I am about to be your family, I can call it how it is." Kandice spun around and headed for the kitchen.

How does Taryn do this all day? This is extremely irritating. Kandice came down the stairs and heard Sam in the office yelling at someone. She crept closer. Quietly, she stood outside the office door. Sam was definitely yelling at someone, but the door was closed, so his voice was muffled. She strained to hear him over the noise of the guests. "Fix the problem now," he ordered. "Did you plant the bomb as requested? THEN DETONATE IT! There can be no evidence."

It got quiet. Kandice, not wanting to be caught, ran to the bathroom and called Alex. The phone rang and rang. Pick up. Pick up. "Hi, you have reached Alex. I am not able to take your call right now, but leave me a message and I will call you back." UGH! On the third try, he picked up the phone.

"What!" he yelled.

"Have you found her?" Kandice asked desperately.

"Yes, but she is badly hurt and unresponsive." Alex snapped. He was very worried and frustrated.

"Get out of there now. There's a bomb some-where! I heard Sam say to detonate..." Kandice was cut off by a loud explosion on Alex's end. "NO!" Kandice screamed. She started to cry. "Alex, can you hear me?" She could hear shout-ing and screaming, but Alex wasn't answering.

She called 911. "Dispatch speaking, can you tell me the location?" a voice came on the line.

"There's been an explosion, and I am not sure where, but the man behind it all is here at Crys-tal Lakes Estate." Kandice sobbed, "You have to get him. I heard him say to detonate the bomb. You have to get here now. I will try to stop him." She was talking so fast the dispatch officer could hardly understand her.

"Ma'am. Calm down. Where are you?"

"At Crystal Lakes Estates," Kandice screamed into the phone. "The killer is here! I am going after him! He can't get away with hurting my best friend." Kandice couldn't believe Taryn was dead, or else she wouldn't have the strength to move forward.

"Ma'am, we will..." The dispatch voice became muffled as Kandice shoved the phone in her pocket and ran to find Sam.

Sam was sitting at the computer when Kandice burst into the office.

"You slimy jerk!" She yelled. "How could you? You blew up my best friend."

"What are you talking about?" Sam leaned back in his chair.

"I heard you tell someone to detonate the bomb. I called my friend and heard the explosion. Taryn was kidnapped and Alex found her. But you blew them up!" She started to sob.

"If your friend hadn't been meddling in matters that didn't concern her, she would still be here. I warned her several times," he said, with a devilish grin on his face. Sam rose from his chair as he spoke.

Kandice felt a surge of hatred and adrenaline as she lunged at him. Sam backed away. She fell forward, catching herself on the edge of the desk. He swiftly appeared behind her, grabbed her by the throat and started squeezing with both hands. He might have looked frail, but he was incredibly strong. Kandice squirmed to get free. His grip only tightened. As he squeezed harder, choking her, he whispered into her ear, "You will be joining her shortly."

As her world was starting to go dark, she remembered her defense training. Kandice flipped her legs up around Sam's neck, performing a flying triangle choke, squeezing his neck tight and pulling on his head. Sam was too shocked to react, and Kandice was too angry to let go. They crashed to the floor. Sam was out cold. She kicked him in the ribs, hard.

"Not if I get you first," she coughed, flipping her hair out of her face and rubbing her throat. Kandice ran out to her car and got a pair of pink fuzzy handcuffs. She ran back to the office and cuffed Sam to the desk. She slapped him on the cheek. "This is not what I usually use these for, but from now on, I'll be keeping a pair close by," she sneered. She straightened her blouse, adjusted the girls, fluffed her hair, and pulled out her phone. Dispatch was still on the line recording the commotion. Before she could say a word, the police sirens were blaring up the driveway. She stepped out of the office and bumped into Marcy.

"What are you doing in there? I have been looking all over for you. The rehearsal was supposed to start ten minutes ago, and Alex isn't here yet." Her eyes got huge. "Why do I hear sirens?"

"It's a long story. You might want to tell your guests to hang tight a bit," Kandice said, pushing past her.

"Hang tight?" Marcy called, glancing into the office to see Sam out cold and chained to the desk. She gasped.

"Or feed them dinner first? Food always keeps people busy, but do whatever floats your boat." Kandice replied, rushing to the front door. There were bigger problems than the rehearsal dinner.

"Whatever floats my boat?" Marcy squeaked, looking pale and bewildered. She stumbled off to find Dan.

Kandice didn't feel bad for leaving Bridezilla in the dark. She felt that Marcy had done nothing all week but pamper herself with massages; she could take care of her guests for a night.

To be honest, Kandice couldn't give a fig about this rehearsal anyway. She had been running on adrenaline, but it was wearing off, and the thought of Taryn dead was too much for her to handle. Her eyes stung with tears. She jerked open the front door and stepped outside as the police were pouring out of their cars. One of the officers yelled, "Miss, please put your hands up where we can see them." Kandice did as she was told. As he approached, she could see 'Ballenger' on his name tag.

"Taryn, is she okay? Did you find the bomb site?" Kandice questioned.

"Calm down, miss. We need to ask you some questions first."

"Please, I need to know."

"I haven't yet," Officer Ballenger said in a tired, gruff voice. "Boys, go on inside," he ordered the other three officers.

"Wait!" Kandice yelled. "There is a wedding rehearsal going on, and the guests know nothing and are not involved; please don't interrupt them. The man you want is handcuffed to the office desk, first door on the right when you enter the house."

"Do what you need to do boys, but be courteous of the party. Okay, Miss, from the beginning," Officer Ballenger sighed. He was too tired for this.

"What's the beginning? How much of this story do you know?"

"Enough for me to want this case closed; how about we start with the 911 call?"

"Okay, I was helping things run smoothly for Bridezilla in there. Your men really do not want to interrupt that rehearsal."

Officer Ballenger looked annoyed.

"Okay, sorry, I'll stay on task. I heard yelling coming from the office, so I went to investigate." Kandice was speed talking, she wanted out of there.

"Something you and your friend do often, as it appears," Officer Ballenger interjected.

"Yes, but only for important things." Kandice said, placing her hands on her hips.

He rolled his eyes and sighed. "Continue..."

"So, I heard Sam yell, 'Fix the problem now. Did you plant the bomb as requested? THEN DETONATE IT! There can be no evidence.' I ran to call Alex to warn him. I knew he was out looking for Taryn. That's why I am here running this stupid party and not saving my friend." Kandice started to cry again. "She's my best friend; we were like sisters!"

Officer Ballenger handed Kandice a tissue. "Take a moment; it's okay, I have friends out there right now too." His eyes softened, and for some reason, she felt the need to hug him. He stiffened back up and gently pushed her away. "Okay, Miss."

She sniffled and continued her story. "I heard the explosion while I was on the line with Alex. I have no idea where they are, but I called 911, told dispatch there had been an explosion, and told them to send someone here too. I didn't want Sam to get away, so I confronted him. He told me he was going to kill me too. He tried to choke me to death. Look at my neck." She pulled the collar of her shirt down. Her neck was bruised and slightly swollen.

"How did you get away?" Officer Ballenger asked, looking very concerned.

"That's the fun part. My current boyfriend is a jujitsu student, pretty high ranking too. He has been teaching me for several months now how to defend myself. I used to take kickboxing before that, so I..."

Officer Ballenger cleared his throat, interrupting again.

"Right, sorry, I kicked his ass and choked him out."

"You said he was handcuffed to the desk. How did you manage that?"

"Well, my boyfriend and I were having some fun role-playing, you know?"

"No, I don't." Officer Ballenger looked uncomfortable.

"You should try it sometime," Kandice winked.

He looked at her again, and this time he smiled. "Is there anything else, Miss?"

"No, just that I will forever keep handcuffs in the car. They have come in handy twice now."

"Thank you, Miss." Officer Ballenger smiled. His radio buzzed, "All persons are being transported to St. Francis Hospital."

"Is that Taryn? I have to go." She jumped up and started to run down the steps.

"Miss, you must wait until we are done here." Officer Ballenger grabbed her arm.

"Please, you have to let me go." Kandice begged.

"Just give us a few more minutes," he replied, letting go of her arm and ushering her towards the house.

Kandice sighed and reluctantly marched into the house. The officers had let the party go on with little interruption. The guests were talking and eating dinner. Everyone looked happy except Marcy, whose eyes had just met Kandice's. She got up, excused herself, and grabbed Kandice by the arm. Before she could say anything. Kandice explained the situation.

"I need to see if Taryn and Alex are alright. You will need to stay and run this by yourself. Tell Dan, he will help you," Kandice said.

Marcy's eyes welled up with tears. "I am so sorry. I was horrible to you, and I should not have been. Go take care of your friend. Dan and I will be at the hospital just as soon as I can get everyone out," she promised.

"I will text you the news once I get there. Ask Mrs. Williams for help; I am sure she would love to."

Marcy hugged Kandice tightly. "Go," she said.

Kandice turned and ran faster than she had ever run. Running was Taryn's thing, not hers. She ran right past the police, who were shoving Sam into a patrol car.

"Wait! Miss!" one of them yelled.

She ignored them, jumped into her jeep, and drove away.

Chapter 20

"This is why you didn't want us to check, isn't it?" Alex screamed out of the trailer at Jake. He was still ripping at the screen keeping him from getting to Taryn.

"No, sir, I had nothing to do with this. I had no idea she was in there," Jake protested, backpedaling as fast as he could.

David grabbed Jake's wrist and slapped a cuff on it.

"Jake, you are under arrest. You have the right to remain silent. Anything you say can and will be used against you," David said as he handcuffed Jake's other hand and sat him down on the side of the road.

David climbed into the trailer to help Alex free Taryn from her musical coffin. The two men cut, hacked, and tore with their bare hands at the piano. It was hammered shut so tightly that it seemed impossible to get to her.

"How did they get her in here?" David asked.

"I don't want to know. I only hope she was out for it," Alex replied, breathing heavily.

Sweat was dripping from his brow, and his hands were a bloody mess by the time they got the last nail out.

"Is she alive?" David asked.

Alex gently touched her, praying she was alive.

"She has a pulse, but it feels weak," he said.

"Help me pull her out."

The two men worked quickly at unfolding Taryn's lifeless body. They pulled her loose just as the ambulance arrived. The EMTs pulled out the gurney, and Alex carried her limp body to them. He didn't want to let her go. A single tear ran down his cheek. He was a tough guy and had seen a lot, but this was almost too much to handle. He had never witnessed someone he loved in this condition before. It didn't feel as though she would make it. He kissed her on the forehead and said a prayer.

The EMTs went to work on Taryn right away, checking her vitals and oxygen intake. They wanted to make sure she was stable before they transported her to St. Francis Hospital. Alex was right; she was alive, but only just.

"Alex, we need to check the other pianos," David called from inside the trailer.

Alex reluctantly climbed back inside, and they started opening every piano. As they worked, the EMTs hollered that they were ready to take Taryn to the hospital. Alex wanted to leave and be with her, but he couldn't leave David alone to deal with this. What if there were more people inside these things? He needed to stay until more help came. He climbed out of the trailer and into the ambulance, squeezed Taryn's hand, and kissed her, hoping she would wake up.

She opened her eyes and whispered, "Alex, I am so sorry."

She started to fade out again but fought just long enough to weakly whisper the name, "Sam."

She was out again. The EMTs shooed him out of the ambulance. They were ready to transport her to the hospital. She was stable for now.

Alex stood and watched them speed away, sirens blaring.

Alex returned to the trailer. He was filled with rage. He tore open piano after piano with David. There were no other bodies. The strings and inside parts had all been removed. It looked like the pianos had been prepped to hide items for smuggling.

"Hey guys, need a hand?" hollered one of the guys from the crime lab. He was a tall, lanky guy named Brandon. His partner was a chubby young man named Matthew. The pair looked like Abbott and Costello.

"The third piano on the right, second row, is where the victim was found. See if you can get any evidence off of it. We will finish checking the others," David ordered, pointing in the general direction.

"Got it," Detective Brandon replied as he saluted David.

"Hey Alex, take a look at this," David pointed inside the second to last piano they had to open.

There were several ammo cans. David took a picture with his phone and then opened the top can. It was full of cash.

"Hey boys," David hollered to the lab guys, "We will need an assembly line to put these cans in the squad car."

He started handing the cans to Alex, who passed them to Matthew and Brandon. The men carried twenty ammo cans full of money to the police car trunk. They would be taken back to the precinct as evidence. The boys continued searching the trailer from top to bottom.

"Hey Detective, come here for a second," Matthew beckoned David over.

"Okay, give me a minute to climb out of here," David hollered back. He turned to Alex, who was still hammering away at the pianos.

"Get to the hospital. I've got help now, and two more officers are on the way. Trust me, if you don't go, you may lose any chance of getting her back if she pulls through."

Alex nodded in agreement. He and David carefully picked their way around broken piano bits and climbed over the larger intact frames. Alex's phone rang twice during the process, but he ignored it. It wouldn't be news of Taryn; they wouldn't even be at the hospital yet. On the third time, Alex finally picked up.

"What!" he yelled into the phone. It was more frustration than anger.

"Have you found her?" Kandice asked.

"Yes, but she is badly hurt and unresponsive," he replied. His tone was much softer.

"Get out of there now. There's a bomb somewhere, I heard Sam say to detonate..."

Alex didn't get to hear the rest of Kandice's sentence. He heard a soft beep as he climbed down from the trailer. His foot had barely touched the ground. He had no time to react. The bomb went off.

The force of the explosion sent all four men flying. Jake blew over like a tumbleweed rolling out of control. The trailer went up in flames; the pianos acted like kindling. It was a massive ball of fire. Alex landed flat on his back a few feet from the trailer. He felt a trickle of blood roll down his face, ears ringing and his arm throbbing with pain. He tried to push himself up, but a rush of dizziness overtook him and the world went black.

Fire trucks, police, and ambulances roared out of Silver Springs. The two officers who had come to help Detective David and his crime lab guys were almost to the scene when the explosion happened. They had called dispatch when they saw the plume of smoke. Kandice's call had come in just seconds after. Matthew and Brandon were mostly unharmed, just a few minor scrapes from being knocked over. They had been behind the squad car with the cases of money. Jake was pretty scraped up from rolling across the pavement but would be okay too.

Officer Braggart and Officer Hicks were first on the scene. David was on the ground right off the bumper of the trailer. He was out cold and had a pool of blood forming around him. Alex lay next to him. The officers raced over to the fallen men. They started work immediately on David. He had a chunk of the metal trailer siding sticking out of his left thigh, and the back of his head had a large gash from hitting the pavement. Alex had a broken arm and a small stitch-worthy cut on the right side of his head at the hairline.

Officer Braggart tore a piece of his own shirt off and tied it like a tourniquet around David's left leg just above the wound to get the bleeding to slow while waiting for the EMTs to arrive. Officer Hicks went over to help Jake off the ground.

"Are you okay, sir?" Officer Hicks asked.

"Yeah, I think I am fine, but I had nothing to do with this, and now my truck is destroyed," Jake lamented.

"I can't un-cuff you and let you go yet. You will be sent to the hospital to be checked out," Officer Hicks said apologetically.

Sirens wailed in the near distance. The EMTs jumped out almost before the ambulance had come to a stop. They rushed to where David and Alex lay. David was hooked up to an IV and immediately loaded into the ambulance, where they continued to work on him. An EMT was checking Alex for more injuries than the obvious. He went to work splinting his broken arm. Alex started to moan and wake up. His head was throbbing.

"Sir, can you stand?" he asked.

"Um, yeah," Alex groaned, sitting up. "What happened?"

"Sir, there was an explosion. You broke your arm and need stitches for the gash on your head. We need to get you to the hospital," the EMT stressed.

The total realization had come over Alex's face. "David, is he okay?" He asked.

"I am not sure, sir, but they are working on him now. I would like to get you into the ambulance with him and take you two to the hospital."

"I need to go," Alex said as he stood up abruptly. His arm, surprisingly, didn't hurt as badly as expected, but his head was a different story. He wobbled a bit.

"I need to get to Taryn. She's not safe. Whoever did this is going to try again." Alex attempted to run to his car but was grabbed by Officer Braggart.

"Wait, Alex! We know who it is. Some woman at Crystal Lakes has him cuffed to a desk. I guess she kicked his ass when she thought he had killed Taryn. He tried to kill her too. We got him. I need you to go to the hospital and get yourself checked out. That arm needs a cast.

Officer Hicks and I can take care of the rest. Once you're rested, we will call you back in. The guy's name is Sam something."

"Taryn tried to say something about him, but she was too weak to talk," Alex replied.

"We have an officer at the hospital ready to talk to her when she wakes up. Now go to the hospital," Officer Braggert demanded.

Alex agreed and was helped into the ambulance. He was still having trouble standing. His head throbbed with pain. When he saw how awful his friend looked, there was nothing he could do but pray. He felt so helpless. They closed the door, and the ambulance took off for the hospital. Alex sat in silence while the EMTs monitored David. He had to fight hard not to doze off. His pounding headache was no doubt a concussion. He knew the EMTs were watching him as well, but he didn't want to distract them from working on David. He had lost a lot of blood. What a horrible nightmare this had become.

Officer Braggert helped Jake into the other ambulance; he looked fine but still needed to be checked out. He sent Officer Hicks with Jake and the crew. Brandon, Matthew, and Braggert stayed at the scene to collect whatever evidence was left. The firemen put out the flames, and tow trucks arrived to help clean up the mess.

Chapter 21

At the hospital, the EMTs rushed David to the operating room. Alex was placed in a wheelchair since he'd likely suffered a concussion. Before they wheeled him through the ER doors, he was asking about Taryn. He needed to see her. He was about to stand up and bolt when a short, little, bubbly ER nurse named Marie gently grabbed his shoulder.

"We can't have you walking around. We need to get you patched up," she said with a smile.

"You don't understand; I need to find Taryn. You can fix me up later," Alex pleaded. He needed to have his head stitched up, a CAT scan of his head, and his arm X-rayed and casted.

"Are you a relative?" Marie asked as she checked his vitals and monitored him from the tiny ER room. They weren't ready for him yet.

"No, I am her boyfriend, well, sort of," Alex explained. He actually didn't know what they were now.

Marie's petite nose wrinkled at the answer. "So... friend, then?" she asked.

Alex reluctantly answered, "Yes."

"I am sorry, sir, but given the nature of how she was brought in, I can't reveal any information," Marie apologized.

"Please, I need to see her; I need to know she is okay," he pleaded. At this point, he was ready to beg if he had to.

The EMT who had brought Taryn in approached Alex. "Thank goodness you found her when you did, man. Things would be quite different if she had been like that much longer," he said, shaking Alex's good hand.

"Is she going to be okay?" Alex asked for what felt like the hundredth time.

"We believe she is going to be just fine. She has a broken ankle, a cut on her forehead that needed stitches, and quite a few scrapes and bruises. They are running tests to make sure nothing else happened to her. It appears as though she has been heavily drugged. She hasn't been able to stay awake long enough to tell us much," the EMT explained.

"Thank you," Alex said.

Marie's brown eyes softened. "You saved her?"

"Yes, I found her stuffed into a piano and got her out just a little before the explosion. I wish I could have saved her sooner," Alex sighed. He felt angry with himself.

"I could lose my job for this, but let's go. This love story needs a proper ending, and that won't happen with you stuck here," she said with a smile.

She wheeled Alex down the hall to the ICU wing where Taryn was being monitored. Room 102, the plaque next to the door said. Two uniformed officers stood guarding the door. Alex knew them; he knew most of the guys at the precinct.

"Hey Alex, is David okay?" one of them asked, looking Alex up and down.

"I don't know; he is in surgery now."

"You don't look so good yourself."

Alex looked down at his arm; it was twice the size of the other and black and blue. He was covered in dirt and blood. He hadn't even thought about his own state of being. He had been so focused on Taryn. His arm throbbed with pain, and his head hurt.

"I'll get fixed up after I see her," he said as he nodded in the direction of Taryn's room.

They opened the door. Taryn lay still in the hospital bed, breathing ever so slightly. The monitors buzzed with stats of her heart rate, blood pressure, and oxygen levels. It was quiet.

Marie pushed Alex's chair as close as she could to Taryn's bedside. Alex gently grabbed her hand and held it for a few minutes, just staring at her. She looked so peaceful, so beautiful, and so helpless. He stood up to kiss her; as he leaned in, their lips met, and she opened her eyes. Her beautiful green eyes stared into his. Welling up with tears, they kissed again.

"I love you," he said, his breath on her lips.

They could hear a commotion in the hall. "Stop!" yelled someone. Several footsteps shuffled about. There was a loud crash at the door, and it burst open. In rushed Robert, followed by the two officers. He ran to the other side of the bed and picked up Taryn's other hand.

"You're okay," he said. He leaned in to kiss her but was grabbed by one of the officers.

"Let's go, buddy; you're not supposed to be in here."

"Hey! I love this woman and she needs me by her side," he said as he jerked away from the officer.

He leaned in and kissed Taryn. She tried to dodge him but didn't have the strength.

Alex stood up and grabbed Robert by the front of his shirt.

"She is not yours to protect."

Marie and the officers escorted both men out of Taryn's room.

"How did you get out of jail?" Alex yelled.

"They released me," Robert smirked, smoothing his shirt and hair.

Alex growled partially because of frustration with Robert and partially because of the pain he was in. Just as they were about to continue their bickering,

Kandice came running up. She was wheezing and gasping for air. Trying to catch her breath, she asked, "Where is she?"

"The room behind us," both men replied in unison. The officers blocked the door. This was becoming a circus.

"I'm her best friend," said Kandice. "You can let me in."

Alex nodded at the officers. "It's true. Hey, Kandice, I need to get fixed up. Keep him away from her," he gestured to Robert.

"No problem!" Kandice punched the palm of her hand and grinned.

Robert sat in a chair outside her room, pouting slightly, but mostly pleased with himself. He saw everything as a win.

"Sweet wheels," he called out to Alex as the nurse wheeled him away. Alex rolled his eyes and huffed.

Kandice pulled a chair close to Taryn. She was sleeping again. They would chat once she was feeling better.

Once back in the ER, Alex got stitched up and was placed in an air cast. He checked on David. David had made it out of surgery and was expected to make a full recovery. The metal had pierced his femoral vein in his left leg, and he had a mild concussion from the impact with the street. It could have been a lot worse. David would stay overnight, and Taryn would too. Alex was released. He called Dan; he had missed the entire rehearsal dinner.

Dan and Marcy had explained to their guests that Taryn and Alex had been in an accident and would be okay. The rehearsal went as planned; everything was set for the real deal tomorrow. Alex was exhausted but couldn't go home to sleep, not with Taryn here. He went to her room. Robert was still sitting outside her door, the two uniforms were still on guard, and Kandice was in an oversized chair, next to Taryn.

"How is she?" he asked, taking a seat.

"She has been sleeping since you left. I haven't even talked to her yet. The nurse, Lindsey, keeps checking her vitals. She seems to be doing fine," Kandice replied softly.

"Do we know anything yet?" he inquired.

"Well, it doesn't look like any physical harm came to her. The injuries appear as though she fell from something. She was drugged with near-lethal doses of roofies and sleeping pills."

"Are you staying tonight?" he asked.

"I want to. I can sleep in the chair; it reclines into a bed."

"I'm going to stay too."

He asked for a roll-away bed, and Nurse Lindsey brought one in.

Robert poked his head in. "Why do you get to stay with her? I have known her longer, and if your friend hadn't held me hostage at the jail, I would have been the one to save her."

Lindsey looked at the group; "If you're going to argue, then you'll all need to leave."

Lindsey was pretty enough, in a plain sort of way. She had dishwater blond hair pulled back away from her slim face. She was average-sized, not too thin and not too fat. She had an air about her that implied she wasn't here to care for the outsiders. She was all about business with her patient.

"I would like a roll-a-way too," Robert insisted.

"We cannot fit another bed in here. You are welcome to sleep on the couch in the visiting area," Lindsey said in annoyance, placing her hands on her hips.

"Fine, but not without telling her good night."

Robert walked into the room, approached Taryn, looked at her, and tears started to well in his eyes.

"Good night, Taryn," he said. He kissed her on the forehead, turned, and walked out.

It was late. Alex started to crawl into bed but remembered that he needed to call Taryn's mother and let her know. It was a call he didn't want to make. After much debating with himself, he did the task and explained the whole thing as best he could to the O'Kelly's. It wasn't long before they showed up.

"Only two at a time," Lindsey said, her voice stern. "And keep it down; she is resting." Lindsey clearly took caring for the sick and injured very seriously. This was probably why she looked so annoyed at the number of people trying to see her patient.

Taryn's mother and father ended up in the bed and chair, leaving the waiting area filled with Alex, Kandice, Robert, and several other O'Kelly's. By morning, Alex's head and arm throbbed, and he needed coffee now. Sleeping mostly upright on a couch next to Robert all night was about as much fun as he could handle.

I groaned. I could hear the steady beeping of the vitals machine. The IV in my arm hurt; as a matter of fact, everything hurt. "Mom, Dad." I whispered. My throat was dry. I motioned for a drink. My mom handed me my hospital-issued water jug, her eyes filled with tears.

"Thank God you are okay," she said, leaning in to hug me.

My dad patted me on my good leg. "You are one tough cookie. I always knew you were," he smiled. I could see the relief in his eyes.

"That Alex of yours is special. He is a hero in my book," Dad smiled.

"Everyone is here waiting to see you. I'll go get them," my mom said and squeezed me one more time.

"She is awake and talking!" Mrs. O'Kelly announced, with tears in her eyes and a smile on her face.

Alex jumped to his feet, followed by Robert and Kandice. They rushed into her room, ignoring the two-person rule. Lindsey was gone now anyway, and there was a new nurse on shift.

"I knew you would find me," I said, looking at Alex. "I knew you wouldn't let them hurt me."

"I wish I would have found you sooner." He held my hand. "I am sorry. You have some busy guardian angels." He smiled.

"You too. I can't believe you were blown up. How bad is your arm?"

"Not bad, it hurts, but nothing like my heart did when I thought you were gone."

He had dirt and bloodstains on his clothes. His rugged handsomeness and words made me start to cry. I wiped the tears away and looked at Robert.

"I heard they arrested you. I never really believed you would do something as awful as murder."

"I shouldn't have been in that jail. I wanted to be out looking for you. The moment I was released, I came straight here to see you," he said sincerely.

"That explains why you look the way you do," I said, smiling.

Robert was always perfectly groomed; he smelled good and dressed well. Today, his clothes were wrinkled, his hair a mess of straw on his head, and he needed to shave or commit to a beard.

"I couldn't leave your side," he smiled. No matter how shabby he looked, that smile was always perfect.

"Kandice kicked Sam's butt yesterday. She figured it out before the rest of us. I guess Lucy and Ethel have a knack for solving mysteries," Alex said.

"I'd prefer a Charlie's Angels reference, thank you! I don't remember Lucy or Ethel ever having handcuffs or choking anyone out! Plus, I much prefer leather to 50s housewife attire," Kandice grinned.

Everyone laughed at that.

"I need a shower," I said.

The new nurse, Rachel, looked stunned. "You just woke up. You're too weak."

"You don't know this girl," Alex and Robert said in unison.

Rachel looked around at the motley crew. "She is going to need some help if I allow this."

"I will," again in unison, the guys replied.

"I can help her," Kandice said.

I would have preferred Alex's help, but given his state, we would have been a disaster.

Rachel sent the boys out. They had decided to get cleaned up as well and would be back quickly. Kandice and Rachel helped me out of bed. The broken ankle was really going to put a cramp in my style. The warm water felt so wonderful. If it weren't for the fact that I really was still very weak, and Nurse Rachel wanted me to make it fast, I could have stood under the warm water for hours. Kandice helped me wash, get dressed in a light blue gingham hospital gown, and into the reclining chair. I didn't want to be back in that bed. I was really rocking the hospital style when Alex showed up with a long pink maxi skirt and matching blouse. He even brought a pair of silver flats. No heels for me for a while.

"Just in case you get released today," he said, smiling. He leaned in and kissed me.

"So does this mean things are good between us again?" I asked.

"Always," he smiled.

I smiled back, feeling more and more like myself. I wanted to go home. I had a wedding to finish, and the sooner I got back to life, the better.

"Now that you're looking much better, I am going to go get cleaned up," Kandice said. "Alex, she's under your supervision now."

"Thank you, Kandice, for everything!" Alex gave Kandice an awkward, one-arm hug. She hugged him back.

My family trickled in and out; most of them had gone home knowing I was safe and should be released soon. My mother wanted to ask questions but was trying her best to pretend nothing had happened. I think she didn't want to upset me. It was nice; I didn't feel like talking about it anyway. I would be soon enough with the police report I was going to have to make. My father watched the news; the trailer explosion was one of the top stories in the nation. I could tell my mother wanted to clean something, but she sat with Alex and me and played cards until enough doctors and nurses had come in to put their stamp of approval on my release. Finally, I was going home.

On our way out, we stopped by David's room. He was going to be fine and would probably be released in the morning. My parents drove us home. This was going to be interesting, with my broken ankle and Alex's arm. Hopefully, Kandice was up for taxiing us places. I could tell my mother did not want to leave me. Alex must have sensed it too, because he let her know that he would be staying with me and would take care of me, on the couch, of course. My father raised an eyebrow suspiciously at Alex, and as if throwing up his hands, he nodded in agreement.

"Keep her safe," he said and escorted my mom out.

I sat down on the couch. A rush of exhaustion came over me. We didn't need to be at Crystal Lakes for another hour and a half.

"I think I will take a short nap," I said to Alex.

"You don't have to go," he said.

"Yes, I do. Part of it's closure, and part of it's me. I didn't plan this beautiful wedding with Bridezilla just to go and miss it."

I closed my eyes and fell asleep on the couch.

Kandice arrived, Trey in tow, an hour later. I fluffed my hair and applied some makeup. Ultimately, I wasn't all that worried about how I looked. You can't make the mess I was in look good, but I didn't want to worry the guests either.

Alex looked great in his tux, but he couldn't get his left arm into his coat. I had to drape it over his shoulder. I don't know how someone could be blown up the day before and still look so damn sexy. Trey and Alex helped me down the stairs and into the car.

"You have one badass girlfriend," Alex said to Trey once in the car.

"I know. She is pretty incredible.

Kandice smiled slyly and said, "In more ways than one."

I could see Trey blush under his dark skin. He smiled back.

I didn't really know Trey as well as I felt I should. He had just appeared in Kandice's life and came and went a lot. She seemed happy, though.

Chapter 22

We arrived at Crystal Lakes Estate with about 10 minutes to spare. Kandice pulled up to the door, and Trey jumped out to help me. Crutches sucked. I hobbled to the door and rang the bell. Mrs. Williams answered the door. She gasped when she saw me, then burst into tears and hugged me.

"You poor dear. I was worried sick when I heard what had happened to you. To think that awful man worked here with me for months and I had no idea," she released me.

"Come in." She moved from the doorway to allow me room to hobble in.

"It's okay," I said. "None of us suspected him."

"I have some freshly baked pumpkin choco-late chip cookies if you would like," she offered as my crutches made the clicking sound crutch-es do on hard floors.

"I would love a cookie. Thank you."

Mrs. Williams is the third-best baker I know. Third only to my mother and grandmother.

We went to the kitchen, and it smelled so delicious. She handed me a cookie; it was melt-in-your-mouth perfect. I started to feel a little creeped outstanding in the same spot where I had found Bambi's body. I had been back in this kitchen several times since that day, but somehow it was different now. I felt nauseous. I needed some air.

"Excuse me, Mrs. Williams, I need some air," I said and hobbled out to the patio.

Once outside, I relaxed, took a deep breath, and exhaled. Someone came up behind me and touched my shoulder. I about jumped out of my skin and nearly fell over my crutches. If it weren't for Alex grabbing me, I would have fallen.

"Whoa, are you alright? I barely touched you, and you freaked out." His eyes betrayed how worried he still was.

"Sorry, coming back here has me more creeped out than I thought it would. I will be okay."

"It looks fantastic out here, you've done a great job.

"Thanks, I think so. This really does look like a fairy tale wedding," I smiled.

Alex leaned in and kissed me. What a mess we were. We were silent, staring into each other's eyes and falling deeper in love. He leaned in for another kiss, his soft lips against mine.

The tranquility was interrupted when I heard a shriek.

"Taryn!" It was Marcy; she was running full speed straight for me. "You're okay! You're alive! Thank heavens!"

I braced myself for impact. Alex must have felt the need too, because he grabbed my arm and squeezed to help steady me. She launched herself at me and hugged me. I rocked a bit but didn't fall over.

"Hi, Marcy," I laughed, giving her a gentle pat on the back.

"We have so much to do! I will be a wife in an hour!" She screeched with enthusiasm.

"I think we are pretty well set," I said.

"Not quite," she said.

Great, it really does never end with this one, I thought.

"What's wrong?" I asked. "It looks to me like everything is just how we planned it." With the exception of murder and kidnapping, I thought.

"I want to change one thing," she said. "You must walk in with Alex!"

"I have things to direct, people to seat, and cues to run."

"Nonsense. We did just fine without you yesterday," she insisted.

"I don't think it's necessary," I said. "This is your moment; I don't need to butt in," I said, trying hard not to hurt her feelings.

"Butt in?! If you hadn't done what you did, we probably wouldn't be here at this moment. I won't hear another word. You will walk in and be announced as the power couple that saved this magnificent wedding, and that is final. The media will love it, and so will I!" she squealed. "I have to finish getting ready. See you shortly!" she said as she scurried off.

Crap, I thought. I didn't want this publicity. Alex put his arm around me. "You knew, didn't you? That's why you chose this outfit, so I would somewhat match the bridesmaids," I accused him.

He grinned, "When Marcy tells you to do something, you do it. Besides, Power Couple sounds fun. I can think of a lot of things a power couple could do together."

"Not in the shape we are in," I huffed. If I could have stormed off, I would have, but frankly, I didn't have the energy or balance on these damn crutches to do so. Dramatic moments will have to wait for another time.

"You're cute when you're frustrated," Alex snickered.

"So I have been told." I rolled my eyes, but couldn't stop a smile from forming on my lips.

The wedding started, and we were announced as Alex and Taryn, "power couple that saves happy endings". Marcy arrived by boat looking like Cinderella awaiting her Prince Charming. The wedding was beautiful, and the reception was grand. At the end of the evening, I was toast. I would like to pretend that Alex carried me up the stairs to his room and made historic love to me. But the reality was he couldn't carry me with his broken arm, and it took me 15 minutes just to get up the stairs. By the time we made it to his room, we both were exhausted. So we settled for snuggling, the best we could in bed. No problem, right? After all, tomorrow is another day!

The End

Thank you so much for reading. I hope you enjoyed the story.
I'd truly appreciate an honest review. Reviews help other readers discover books they might love, and they mean more to authors than you know.
For your convenience, you can
visit SaltyInspirations.com/books/ or scan the QR code below to leave a review.

About the author

Michelle L. Clifton was raised in southwest Colorado in the great valleys of the Rocky Mountains. There, she married the love of her life and raised two beautiful kids, along with a cat, two dogs, and a flock of chickens.

Over the years, Michelle has worked in the dental field, the dance and theater industry, athletics, and event coordinating. She created *Salty Inspirations* to pursue her passion for writing, though her favorite job will always be being Mom.

Her family made a major move to Cape Coral, Florida, just in time for Hurricane Ian. These days, they split their free time between hiking and camping in Colorado and boating and beaching in Florida.

Oh, and writing, of course!

Connect with Michelle

Visit me online at Saltyinspirations.com

Love mystery, mischief, and exclusive bookish perks? Sign up for my monthly newsletter for the latest updates on the Taryn O'Kelly Mysteries, upcoming events, sneak peeks, and freebies just for subscribers!

Follow me here:
Facebook/authorMichelleLClifton
Instagram
Michelle L Clifton @ salty_inspirations_
YouTube/saltyinspirations
Pinterest/saltyinspirations
Goodreads/MichelleLClifton

Acknowledgements

Taryn, Alex, Kandice, and Robert would never have come to life without my husband's constant encouragement, support, and belief in me. He gently pushed me every step of the way while we raised our two kids. When the book was finally finished, he eagerly read it, mysteries aren't his usual reading material. Yet he was excited to see what I had worked on for so many years while teaching and managing the kids. He is truly the love of my life.

My daughter and line editor, Taegen Clifton, inspired me to publish this book. Her passion for reading, constructive criticism, and hilarious editing notes made reworking parts of the story a joy. For years she wanted to read it, but I felt she was too young. She patiently waited, became a line editor, and finally read the book, what a thrill!

My son, who is always sending me marketing ideas, has contributed positive energy and insightful input that made this journey possible.

My mother and editor, Shauna Blaylock, with her incredible ability to spot even the smallest grammatical error, has ensured this book is an enjoyable, polished work of fiction.

To all my family and friends who have believed in me and my book, thank you! I hope you enjoy reading it as much as I loved writing it.